SECRETS
OF THE
CASA
ROSADA

SECRETS
OF THE
CASA
ROSADA

Alex Temblador

PIÑATA BOOKS
ARTE PÚBLICO PRESS
HOUSTON, TEXAS

Secrets of the Casa Rosada is funded in part by a grant from the Texas Commission on the Arts. We are grateful for their support.

Piñata Books are full of surprises!
An Imprint of Piñata Books

Arte Público Press
University of Houston
4902 Gulf Fwy, Bldg 19, Rm 100
Houston, Texas 77204-2004

Cover design and photograph by Victoria Castillo

Names: Temblador, Alex, author.
Title: Secrets of the Casa Rosada / by Alex Temblador.
Description: Houston, TX : Piñata Books, an imprint of Arte Público
    Press, [2018] | Summary: Sixteen-year-old Martha's life is transformed
    when her mother leaves her in Laredo, Texas, in 1990 with a
    grandmother she never knew, who is a revered curandera.
Identifiers: LCCN 2018029355 (print) | LCCN 2018036171 (ebook) |
    ISBN 9781518505492 (epub) | ISBN 9781518505508 (kindle) |
    ISBN 9781518505515 (pdf) | ISBN 9781558858701 (alk. paper)
Subjects: | CYAC: Grandmothers—Fiction. | Healers—Fiction. | Mexican
    Americans—Fiction. | Secrets—Fiction. | Blessing and cursing—
    Fiction. | Family life—Texas—Fiction. | Texas—History—20th
    century—Fiction.
Classification: LCC PZ7.1.T444 (ebook) | LCC PZ7.1.T444 Sec 2018
    (print) | DDC [Fic]—dc23
LC record available at https://lccn.loc.gov/2018029355

♾ The paper used in this publication meets the requirements of the American
National Standard for Information Sciences—Permanence of Paper for
Printed Library Materials, ANSI Z39.48-1984.

Printed in the United States of America
September 2018–October 2018
Versa Press, Inc., East Peoria, IL

5 4 3 2 1

Table of Contents

Acknowledgements

While writing this book, I worked through a lot of emotions and thoughts surrounding my identity, and though it was a personal journey, it would not have been possible without the help of quite a few individuals. I want to offer a special thanks to the following people:

Rilla Askew, for her mentorship and guidance throughout the writing, editing and pitching process and reminding me that this story needs to be told and heard. Connie Squires whose excitement for my novel never waned after she read my book for the first time; thank you for believing in my novel and telling me it deserved to be published.

Angela Morris and Amy Little, my best pen pals and writing partners. I highly regarded your edits and critiques, as you always had my best interest at heart. I wouldn't have made it here without you, and I hope we continue to support each other.

My cousin, Steven "Severo" Gonzalez for sharing his experiences with a *curandera* with me, which helped me craft the *curanderismo* practice portrayed in the book.

My Laredo family for welcoming me with open arms, my cousin Richie for showing me around the city, and to the city of Laredo for providing a wonderful place to set my novel.

Uncle Andy for printing out my books and stories over the years, so I could have something to touch and edit. To hold your book in your hands is to hold hope.

To the countless readers over the years who provided feedback, suggestions and edits—I took every praise, every critique, every suggestion to heart. Thank you.

My grandma for being the inspiration for the character of Abuela and my Meme for inspiring the character of Gloria. I love and miss you both.

My dad for reading every single chapter and offering wonderful feedback, my mother for sharing my book news with all, my sister for being my confidante, hero and inspiration, and my brother for always believing and loving me.

With love, I thank you all.

To my family, for being my support, readers and inspiration.

Uno

WHEN I ARRIVED IN LAREDO, TEXAS, during a late August afternoon in 1990, the houses were painted in shades of mustard yellow, baby blue, dark red, light green, dingy brown or a white color that had yellowed around the edges. I remember it well because it reminded me of a bad Andy Warhol painting. I had looked over Warhol's work in the Memphis library only weeks before and, there I was, a sixteen-year-old girl driving through a shabby version of one his creations.

The ridiculously colored dwellings were caged in with wrought-iron fences spread between squared cinder block or brick posts. My mother and I drove through a sea of yellow grass, brown, scraggly bushes, palm trees, large, spiky plants and cacti. The scorched lawns of the houses came all the way to the street, leaving no room for sidewalks in the neighborhood.

Paint peeled down the sides of many houses in long, jagged strips. Bent chain-link fences hung orange and brown with rust. Basketball rims with wooden headboards from the '50s stood in the street without their nets alongside broken-down cars with missing hubcaps. We drove past a cemetery with hundreds of tombstones, each one covered in elaborate displays of floral arrangements and ribbons.

At the age of sixteen I wasn't very impressed with Laredo, especially not with the neighborhood where my grandmother lived. As my mother and I drove on the rocky asphalt roads in our maroon Pinto, the pit in my stomach widened. We drove from the real world—what I knew as America—into another country, one that did not fit with my notion of what a U.S. city looked like.

Commercial businesses were being built along the main highway, but they were tire stores, local restaurants and clothing stores with names that I didn't recognize—many had Spanish names.

My mother and I had never lived in a house. Our "homes" consisted of cheap, moldy, one-bedroom apartments on the run-down side of town . . . if we were lucky. The times we weren't lucky, we stayed in carpet-stained, moth-eaten-sheets kind of hotels with drug deals going down in the rooms next to us. Our neighbors had been mostly black or white with a few Hispanics from Puerto Rico or Cuba mixed in.

Despite this—or maybe even because of it—I had a grand idea of what houses should look and feel like. They were in magazines, on television and in movies: houses were supposed to be made out of rusty red to light tan bricks, complete with tan, white or gray siding, and lush, green evenly mowed lawns. You could practically smell the fresh paint job, and the sidewalks that ran in front of the houses were being used by neighbors walking their dogs or kids riding their bicycles.

But that was not Laredo in 1990.

Little children played on the lifeless lawns while their brown mothers seemed to melt in the heat on plastic green and white lawn chairs. Men stood in groups, some with their shirts off, displaying black hairy chests tattooed with symbols and words that made my heart beat faster in fear. Others wore bandanas, and even the older men with salt-and-pepper hair stood on porches or on the lawns with beer bellies and hard eyes, watching our car as we passed.

We were a few blocks from my grandmother's house when we halted at a stop sign that had black symbols spray-painted on it, none of which meant anything to me. Four men stood at the corner talking among themselves, but all at once they stopped to look at our Pinto. Their eyes stared through our cracked windshield, glaring at us, as if they knew we were not from Laredo . . . at least not me. They stood closest to *my* door, the one that never locked. I reached out slowly and held onto the handle, a naïve action, because if they rushed the car, I didn't stand a chance.

Everything about the men put me on edge:their slicked-back black hair complimented their black mustaches and goatees, three wore stained wife-beaters with jeans and had tattoos up and down their arms. The oldest of the bunch—by some forty years—wore a gray work shirt that he left unbuttoned to expose an oil-stained T-shirt. The one closest to my door smiled mischievously and took a step forward. At that same time my mother's foot finally found the gas and we left the men behind.

When the men were a block behind us, I turned to my mother and asked, "Is this safe?"

She laughed. "Is what safe, darling?"

"Is this . . . this area safe to be in?"

"Of course it is, Martha. You always ask this." Her voice rose in a mocking manner: "'Is Memphis safe?' 'Is Orlando safe?'" She huffed. "You really need to calm down. Your grandmother wouldn't live somewhere unsafe." Black sunglasses with silver rims hid her eyes as she smiled in a reassuring way. I wanted to barf.

Whatever. I leaned forward and adjusted the air-conditioning vent so that the cool air hit my sweaty face. I missed Memphis and its 97-degree weather. Memphis was like an igloo compared to Laredo's 112-degree heat wave. I peeled my sweat-soaked shirt off my chest so that some air could make its way through the cotton and to my burning skin.

"I can't believe you grew up here," I said.

"What was that, honey?"

"Nothing."

My mother shrugged, leaned forward and turned the music up. It was the only station that she could find that played some pop crap and not Mexican music. I slouched back in my seat and stared at the dashboard, trying not to look around at the next crappy city where we were going to live.

It was difficult to imagine my mother living in a place so . . . Mexican. With her Family Dollar-dyed blonde hair, her light skin and her inch-thick layer of make-up, she had worked hard to look as white as possible. She even refused to walk in direct sunlight for fear her skin would darken.

That day, my mother wore a tight red spaghetti-strap top that stopped just above her navel. Her boobs bounced up and down, ready to fall out of her tight top as she danced to a Madonna song. Her jean shorts were shorter than mine and hugged her butt tighter than a child could hug its mother. Below, her feet were encased in bright red heels. Someone had a funny sense of humor placing me with this woman.

"How much farther?" I asked.

"Just down the street. You're going to love meeting your grandmother."

A week earlier, my mother had come into our kitchen while I was drawing hands for my art class and announced that we were going on a "vacation." We were going to visit my grandmother, whom I had never met before. She made it sound like a fairy tale, and I was Little Freaking Red Riding Hood. She started chatting on and on about how much fun it would be and how I would *love* Laredo. I knew it was her way of keeping me from asking questions: *Have we been evicted again? What do you mean I have a grandmother?* After a few minutes, I stopped listening.

We never stayed longer than two years in one place, moving from city to city. I had five spiral notebooks with drawings and scribbles chronicling the places we had stayed. My mother wanted to be rich, so we moved to any city where she thought she could do that: Atlanta, Boston, Memphis. . . . I'm sure we had moved a lot more in the years after I had been born, I just couldn't remember. My youth consisted of moving from school to school, and friends were far and wide. I never owned more than could fit in my one large suitcase, which always sat next to my bed filled to the brim with all my clothes.

We definitely weren't visiting my grandmother because my mother thought she could become rich in Laredo. I was sure we'd been evicted from our apartment in Memphis and didn't have the money to go anywhere else. Memphis hadn't been as successful for my mother as she had hoped. Waitressing part-time at a local diner never helped much financially barely paid for bills, and her boyfriends—musicians mostly—didn't either. We had slept in our car in parks and campsites, on the way here;

we had changed and washed up in gas stations that had rusty rings around the sinks, stained floors and blackened toilet bowls. I didn't smell good, and my hair looked greasy from a lack of wash, which was only made worse from the dirty water I had to run through it at the last gas station.

My mother continued chatting. I tuned in halfway to something she said: " . . . she's a very sweet woman. Although she can't speak English, she can underst—"

"Who can't speak English?"

"Your grandmother, but she can understand you."

"What do you mean?"

"I mean, she doesn't speak English," she repeated.

"So how the hell am I supposed to understand her? I can't speak Spanish."

She flipped her wrist in a backhanded manner, which made me grit my teeth in annoyance. That movement could be translated to many things: "Don't worry" or "You're crazy" or "No big deal" or "Oh, stop!" I wanted to slap her hand every time she did it.

"It's so easy, and you're so smart. You'll pick it up in no time." She thought flattery would make me feel better about anything. She used it so much that it had lost its power long ago, just like that damn smile she gave me.

My mother had this smile—the "Big Fake." It annoyed the hell out of me. She did it when I was little, and for a while it worked, but as I got older I saw it for what it was, a lie. The Big Fake consisted of her lips rising as far as they could, making her cheeks pop out like a chipmunk's full of nuts. Her shiny, white teeth would sparkle in contrast to her dark lipstick, and each time I had to hold back a gag. She used it on everyone, not just me. Each time she did, I saw the quiver at the edge of her lips, shaking more and more. She hated the Big Fake more than I did.

We turned onto Garfield Street. A few minutes later the car slowed down. We parked behind a gold Cadillac. I sat up in my seat and looked out the window.

"She lives here?"

My mother didn't smile, but only stared at the house before giving a slight nod.

"You're kidding me, right? My grandmother lives in a Pepto-Bismol-colored house?"

She nodded again.

God, it explained so much—like my mother's preference for outrageously bright colors for clothes.

The pink paint, even chipped and faded, made the house stand out bright and loud next to the blue and brown houses on either side of it. Despite its humorous coloring, it called for attention and respect. Even the houses next to it seemed to be leaning ever so slightly towards its wooden frame. I looked up and down the street. None of the houses, as far as I could see, were pink like the one in front of us. Why would someone voluntarily paint their house that color?

My mother stepped out of the car, not waiting for me to get over my astonishment. After she shut her door, she stretched, pushing her breasts and butt out at the same time. You would have thought she did it for an audience, but the only people I saw around were two old ladies sitting on a porch on the opposite side of the street.

I slipped on my sandals and followed her. The intensity of the sun and heat slammed into me as soon as I stepped out of the car. It was 5 p.m. and still broiling? My mother had already moved to the trunk and begun pulling out my suitcase. I prayed to God that the person I found inside would not be an older version of the person I had been stuck with for the last sixteen years.

I reached into the trunk to grab one of mother's suitcases when she batted my hand away.

"We'll come back for mine later. I want you to meet your grandmother now."

"But . . . "

She ignored me and shut the trunk. "I'll get it later, honey. We're wasting time."

Behind us, a door slammed. We both turned to my grandmother's house. A girl around my age, maybe sixteen, or seventeen, wearing an oversized white T-shirt and blue jeans, made her way down the porch steps. Who was she? My mother stopped moving beside me.

The girl finally noticed us, stopped and stared. Her body stiffened. Her hands, which were at her sides, curled into fists. Her eyes darkened until it appeared that only black filled the white spaces. She was breathing heavily, boiling with anger. She looked over her shoulder at the house, then back at me full of malice. I flinched. She noticed, and it made her smile—a small upturn of the corners of her lips. After a moment, she stomped through the open gate and down the street, leaving me with an uneasy feeling.

My mother and I continued to watch the girl in silence. When the girl turned the corner and we weren't able to see her anymore, the spell broke and I was able to move.

"Who was that?" I didn't even know the girl, and yet the hate that had emanated from her eyes had turned me cold in the sweltering heat.

"I don't know." For once, her voice didn't sound fake. Her forehead wrinkled in confusion as she continued looking at the place where the girl had disappeared.

I waved my hand in front of her face. "Hello?"

She blinked out of her trance and turned to me with the Big Fake. There was my mother.

"C'mon, let's get out of this sun. I can feel my skin turning brown."

As we walked up the steps to the cement porch, cramps assaulted my stomach. My mother had never spoken a word about her family before the day she told me we were going to visit my grandmother. For so long, I thought my mother and I were alone.

Questions ran through my mind. *What would my grandmother look like? Would I look like her? Would she like me? Would we be welcomed or left on the porch homeless? Did she even know about me?* But I didn't have time to think about what was about to occur because my mother sat my suitcase down on the porch, opened the screen door and knocked. I stood behind her, a bit toward her right. I pulled one of the short pieces of hair that had fallen in my face behind my ear, even though I never put my hair behind my ears.

The porch was relatively small and felt crowded with all the potted plants on it. How had they not withered and died in the excruciating heat? Then again, I had seen an orange tree in the small courtyard, and it didn't look dead. The plants bloomed in varying shades of green and yellow, and some even sported small clusters of flowers.

During my overview of the plants, I noticed a glass bowl with water sitting next to the door. Three limes floated on the surface.

"What's with the limes?" I asked my mother.

She looked down to where I pointed and pursed her lips. "That's not good."

"What's not good?"

The knob on the front door turned and I forgot about the heat, the plants, the limes. The door opened a few inches, an old woman's head appeared behind the screen. I peered around my mother to get a better look, but the screen door obscured the woman's face. She muttered something in Spanish that I didn't understand.

"Mamá!" My mother said before she released a rampant flow of foreign words.

The woman opened the door a little more and peered around my mother. She nodded toward me with her head and then turned to my mother and said something in Spanish. My mother replied with more alien words, but somewhere in the flow I caught my name. The woman shook her head back and forth and turned slowly away. She left the door wide open as she walked into the house. My mother opened the screen door, picked up my suitcase and entered. She turned to see if I followed.

"Goodness, Martha, stop standing there. Get inside."

"Since when do you speak Spanish?"

I had never heard my mother utter one word in Spanish my whole life, not even to the Puerto Rican and Cuban staff she used to work with at diners. And here she was, speaking as if it had been a daily practice. How could she have kept this secret from me? Instead of answering, she ignored me and disappeared into the house. I caught the screen door before it closed, released a huff of anger and followed her in.

As soon as I stepped through the door, I was overcome by a variety of odors. A mixture of something
spicy and hot and a hint of musk, like the house hadn't
been aired out in years. It took my eyes a few moments
to adjust to the dim lighting. I found myself standing in
a small living room. On the opposite wall sat an old yellow couch with a brown coffee table in front of it. A shag
carpet covered the floor. It might have been brown or a
light brown and had darkened over the years with dirt
and wear.

Next to the couch sat a blue, oscillating fan that
pushed the hot air around the room. Another one sat in
the far right corner. Tiny figurines, plates with pictures
of angels, God, Jesus and Mary littered every shelf and
table, even the floor. I stood in a small, Christian shrine.
I looked around trying to take in every little object—a
three-foot wooden statue of Mary holding a baby Jesus
in the corner, the quilted blanket that lay folded on the
corner of the couch, the many-colored candles halfway
melted in their decorative holders.

My mother's voice interrupted my inspection of the
house. "Martha, come into the kitchen. I want you to
meet your grandmother. And close the door, you're letting the heat in!"

The heat was already in the house. I expected to be
hit by the cold from an air conditioner as soon as I
stepped in, but found ten-year-old fans instead, and they
didn't do much to cool the house down. Regardless, I
turned and pulled the door closed. I would have locked
it, but there wasn't anything to lock.

My focus went to the doorway that my mother had
disappeared through. Sunlight streamed into the dimly
lit living room, causing the miniature, crystal statues on

a table to sparkle. I couldn't walk through. My grandmother was in the kitchen. My grandmother, a woman I
had never met. My doubts had returned and had frozen
my feet. My mother spoke on the other side. If my
grandmother responded, I didn't hear.

I took a deep breath and the ice that froze my feet
melted a little. *You got this, Martha.* My heart beat faster
and faster as I walked through the doorway and into the
kitchen. I don't know what I expected, but it wasn't the
burning smell of chilies. My eyes watered a bit, and
through the tears I had my first look at the kitchen.

It had been painted a sunny yellow—a yellow kitchen
in a Pepto-Bismol house. Everything in it had been painted varying shades of yellow: the walls, the chairs, the
table, the cabinets—even the little hand towels were
white and yellow. The only non-yellow things in the
kitchen were the worn-out tan, floor tiles, the white
linoleum counters and a large, square-shaped, white fan
that sat on the table and blew a warm breeze.

During my overview of the kitchen, I spotted a few
green peppers on a cutting board on the counter. A knife
lay beside the board, just used and dotted with the seeds
of the peppers. Strings of red and orange chili peppers
hung on the opposite wall. Next to the chilies stood a
door with a window from which the evening light shone.
More pots filled with odd-looking shrubs and trees
crowded around the door, making the kitchen appear
smaller than it already was.

My mother, who leaned against one of the kitchen
counters, broke the silence. "Honey, this is your *abuela*,
María." She gestured to the tiny brown woman sitting in
a yellow chair in front of me. Her hands were clasped in

her lap and her lips were pursed as she watched my mother with suspicious eyes.

"My what?" I asked.

My mother laughed nervously. "Your grandmother, honey. *Abuela* means grandmother. Your first Spanish word." She gave me the Big Fake and gestured once more to the lady in front of me.

Even though my mother said it slowly, I couldn't have repeated it back if someone had asked me to. My brain clouded out the Spanish, leaving me without a word to grasp onto.

As I turned from my mother to my grandmother, my palms began to sweat at my sides. The woman in front of me stood up and appeared to be studying me. I didn't know whether to say hello or to give her a hug, although I didn't really want to do that. She was a stranger. She walked toward me, stopping a foot away.

My grandmother didn't reach my shoulders. I had to be more than a foot taller than her and her stocky figure made her appear even shorter. Her large breasts stretched against her thin, white blouse, and her large thighs stretched her orange pants tight. She tilted her head to study my face, and as she studied mine, I studied hers.

Her dark brown skin stood in stark contrast to her long, white hair, twined into a single French braid down her back. Her bushy eyebrows were the same color, and went every which way. As she studied me, she sucked on her teeth, and as she did this, her wrinkles moved up and down, revealing pale, crisscrossed lines between her wrinkles where the sun hadn't tanned.

My mother had a small, button nose. I had always wondered if I had inherited my father's nose, but looking at my grandmother now, I discovered the truth: she and I both had the same long, slender nose with a round tip and a small hook on the end. She even had a few age spots covering the bridge of her nose—the same place my freckles covered. She and my mother shared the same lips: small in width and slightly pointed at the peaks. Unlike my grandmother, my mother smeared hers with cheap, red lipstick. My grandmother's eyes were the only pretty thing about her. The irises, honey brown, shone with youth and knowledge.

I guess she had finished studying my face, because she began to waddle around me, looking me up and down. I felt like a prized pig on display for a purchaser. I turned to my mother behind me and mouthed: *What is she doing?* Luckily my grandmother's height kept her from seeing. My mother batted her hand at me as if to say, "Don't worry." I rolled my eyes and turned around to find that my grandmother had finished. She gave me one last look, her right eye squinting as if she could see me better that way, and then she mumbled something in Spanish under her breath. She shuffled over to the peppers, picked up the knife and began chopping.

I turned around, confused at my grandmother's behavior. My mother whispered to sit down. I let out a sigh and walked to one of the chairs. A hollow feeling grew in my gut.

My grandmother didn't even speak to me. I felt like something to be measured or studied. Did she not like what she saw? And why didn't she speak to me or hug me or something? I didn't think grandmothers behaved this way the first time they met their granddaughters.

My mother, without noticing my hurt feelings, spoke to my grandmother in Spanish. While she continued to chop her peppers. She never once looked at my mother. When my grandmother replied, her tone suggested that she didn't care one way or another about whatever my mother said. My mother's voice rose and she began to speak faster. She sounded like an angry woodpecker compared to my soft spoken, nonchalant grandmother. At one point my grandmother even put down her knife and flicked her wrist backwards at my mother making a *psht* sound. I almost dropped dead. My mother had inherited that gesture from her own mother. I held onto my hand in fear that I would begin to do the same.

My mother actually grew quiet when my grandmother made that sound. I watched as she took a deep breath and controlled her anger. She looked once more at the old woman and pleaded for something in Spanish. I assumed she begged my grandmother to let us stay. My grandmother replied tersely. I grew impatient and a little bored with the exchange. I wanted a shower, a bed to fall asleep in and something to eat. My stomach growled at the thought of food.

My grandmother's response silenced my mother. She nodded her head *Okay* and then pushed herself off the counter. I stood up immediately.

Great, we were going to have to sleep in our car in Little Mexico. I couldn't wash my hair in another gross gas station bathroom! I never cried, but I felt like crying then. Earlier I had thought this small house unsafe in a scary neighborhood, it now appeared to me as a four-star hotel.

My mother plastered the Big Fake across her face, but it faltered when she looked at me. "Honey, you look scared." She rubbed the top of my arm.

"What are you doing?"

She drew her hand back and crossed her arms beneath her chest.

"We're leaving, right?" I asked.

"No, of course not. Your grandmother is excited to get to know her granddaughter. And she's making a special dinner just for you!" The corner of her lips rose, as if she thought smiling bigger helped.

"I doubt that," I muttered.

"Well, believe it, honey. You and your grandmother are going to become *so* close. Now, you sit down. I'm going to go use the ladies room."

"You didn't need to announce that."

I sat back down in the chair. With a smirk still on her face, she backed up toward a doorway I assumed opened to a hallway to the rest of the house. I had to do a double take, because she wasn't giving me the Big Fake anymore. Her smile almost looked genuine. Which freaked me out.

"What?" I said.

"Nothing, honey. Love you." She winked and disappeared through the doorway.

It always made me uncomfortable to hear my mother say the 'L' word to me. I glanced over at my grandmother, who still stood with her back to me. Something had changed: she had stopped chopping. She still clutched the knife, but her head hung down and her body had stilled. Then after a moment, she took a deep breath. Her back rose and, when she released the breath, she began to chop the peppers again.

I watched my grandmother as she continued to cook, suppressing all the uneasy feelings that assaulted me. I sat quietly in my chair, unsure if my grandmother even knew I sat behind her.

When she finished chopping the peppers, my grandmother stood on her tiptoes, opened a cabinet and pulled out a jar of white rice. She shuffled to the stove, which already had a large pot sitting on it. She sat the rice down and turned one of the knobs. From a pocket, she pulled out a match, lit it and placed it by the burner, allowing it to catch fire. I had never seen a stove that wasn't electrical. My mother never cooked anyway, and at an early age, I became a protégé of the microwave. My grandmother's kitchen lacked that magical food cooker, which made me a little uneasy. Regardless, I continued to watch my grandmother with something like fascination, since no one had ever really cooked for me or in front of me. She poured some rice into the pot, pulled a wooden spoon from a drawer and moved the rice around with it.

After watching her tend to the rice my attention wandered around the kitchen. Bright sunlight poured in through a window. It almost made me forget the stark, scary neighborhood that surrounded the house. For a moment, I felt safe with this stout woman, until the silence was broken by some shouts in Spanish, the slamming of a car door and the screech of tires on the road.

I jumped in my chair as my heart sped up. Yeah . . . safe my ass. If I didn't get attacked by a creepy Mexican guy, I'd sure as hell get run over. My grandmother didn't look up or hesitate at the sound, just continued to brown the rice.

It took my grandmother pouring the tomato sauce, water and spices into the pot for the realization to hit me. I wanted to stand up and march around demanding answers. I watched my grandmother pull out a bowl of already cooked chicken from the fridge, tear it into pieces and throw the pieces into the boiling pot. Her calm movements only infuriated the storm within me.

It had been long enough already. I knew this day would come sometime in my life, I just never expected it to be then. I thought it would be my decision, not my mother's. The too-many times the thought had entered my mind before, I had locked it away. Things might have been easier for me if I hadn't been in denial, but perhaps they weren't meant to be easier.

It wasn't until my grandmother sat a plate of rice and chicken and a mug of white milk in front of me, that everything came together, that I allowed the truth to hit me, gave it permission to cut right through me. The slammed door, the car, the screech, the yell, the Big Fakes, the "Love you," her suitcases.

Suddenly, my hunger vanished.

Dos

BLACK EYES, pain in my chest, no air. I clawed at my throat to no avail. I couldn't breathe. Darkness bearing down on me. Skin on fire. I raked my nails across my skin trying to push the flames away. Her finger pointed at me and her black eyes stared me down. Her midnight-colored hair whipped around her head in a fiery wind. Then, through the tornado of flames, she yelled words in a language that made my skin crawl, and with the last foreign sound that slipped from her mouth, I screamed—my body buried in fire.

I jolted awake to the smell of onions and my own sweat. My breath came out in gasps, and I couldn't get enough air. Those eyes, that girl from the porch; for someone I had only seen for a few moments, she had stuck with me to the point that she showed up in my dreams. After a few minutes I calmed down, and then my real life nightmare hit me. It was dark, early Saturday morning. Only eight or so hours after my mother had abandoned me to my grandmother, a total stranger, in Laredo.

Why the hell would she freaking leave me here? Gave me the Big Fake all day! I should have known she was up to something. I wanted to scream and punch the bed over and over and imagine it was her face with its stupid,

19

red, lipstick and stupid, pale skin and then tear out her
fake, blonde hair and show everyone what a real bitch
she was. Who leaves their daughter with a stranger? It
wasn't like I was a burden—I took care of her, mostly. I
didn't want to be here with some Mexican lady who did-
n't speak English. I'd rather suffer my mother's fake-
bull-shitting self.

Placing both of my hands on my forehead, I squeezed
hard trying not to think about what had happened yesterday, but not trying to think about it only made me
think about it more. I needed a distraction.

I sat up, looked around the bedroom and almost
dropped dead. Easter egg purple walls? Really, Grandma? At the foot of the bed, three candles burned on a
small dresser, giving off a faint glow in the tacky-colored
room. A blue candle had been placed at the top, a red
candle on the left side and a green candle on the lower
right corner. Something round sat in front of the candles,
but I couldn't see what it was from the bed.

Small, gold and brown picture frames surrounded the
candles. Most of the pictures were of Jesus and Mary,
but there were a few black and white photographs of
people I didn't know. Crosses hung above the doorway
and over the closet door to the left of the bed.

I fingered the fringe on the four blankets that covered me. No wonder I had been sweating. My grandmother must have placed these blankets on me after I
had fallen asleep. No air-conditioning in this house, and
she thought four blankets was a good idea? I shoved
them to the foot of the bed but left the sheet covering my
legs.

The tendrils of sleep spread through my body again,
my bad dream and real-life nightmare mostly gone from

my thoughts. I let myself fall backwards toward the pillow, but what I saw on the wall above me made me jump back up.

"Holy shit!" I scrambled to the edge of the bed.

Bloodied feet nailed to wood, and the somber face of a man dripping with blood peered down at me. The pale face and tears shone bright in the dark room. Hanging above the bed was the largest cross I had ever seen. It was porcelain or a hard plastic, something shiny. Jesus hung on a four-and-a-half-foot-tall cross, his pale arms stretched two feet wide. The thick rivulets of blood flowed down his cheeks and over the contours of his angular face. The artist had thought it best to add the gruesome ripping of his flesh around the head of the nails.

Weren't religious items supposed to be comforting? Jesus Loves You and all? Suddenly, the room felt cold, and I pulled the blankets back over me. I decided to sleep on the far end of the bed for the rest of the morning in case Jesus fell on me. I could see the headlines now: Death by Jesus.

The onion smell grew stronger now that I sat at the end of the bed. I searched for the culprit until I finally found a small, purple onion that had been cut in half and placed against a picture of Mary. A cross had also been carved out of the onion. That nervous feeling that had begun in my stomach grew more and more. Who was this woman my mother had left me with? For that matter, where *was* my mother?

I laid my head on the crook of my arm as salty tears pooled beneath my eyelids.

I couldn't stop them.

It was the onion.

I swear.

A loud thud shattered my deep sleep, and I awoke to my grandmother hauling my suitcase into the room. She leaned over and placed her hands on her knees, gasping for air.

I sat up and rubbed my eyes. "What are you doing? I could have brought that in. What time is it?"

When my hand dropped back to the bed, it landed on something. I grabbed the object and brought it close to my face. A lemon? I turned to my grandmother and raised it up.

"What's this for?"

My grandmother finally stood back up, her breathing returned to normal. She looked as she had before, white French braid and all. The only difference was her clothes. She had on blue capris and a plain yellow shirt that buttoned in the front.

She squinted at my hand. "Ah!" Holding one finger up, she turned and left the room.

The yellow skin of the lemon sparkled in the soft light. *Wait a minute . . .* my attention turned to the table at the end of the bed. The candles still burned and the wax hadn't melted any lower. I must have fallen asleep for only a few minutes, even though it had felt like hours.

My grandmother returned to the room a few minutes later with a bowl in hand. She came and stood at the foot of the bed and said something to me in Spanish.

"I don't know Spanish, remember?"

She made a frustrated noise deep in her throat. She pointed to my hand that held the lemon and pointed at the bowl.

"You want me to put the lemon in the bowl?" I placed it in the bowl.

"*No. No,*" she scolded then continued spitting out more words.

"You said to put the lemon in the bowl?" Good God, this was becoming ridiculous. I just wanted to sleep.

She grabbed the lemon and held it out to me. I reached with my right hand to take the lemon, but she shook her head. She nodded to my other arm. Why the hell did it matter? I slowly reached out with my left. She pushed the lemon into my hand. Then before I could ask what to do, she grabbed my wrist and yanked it over the bowl. She turned my hand over so that the lemon was closest to the bowl, then placed her hand directly over mine and squeezed.

"Hey!"

She didn't stop but kept squeezing my hand until the lemon was crushed beneath our grips and the juice spilled onto my palm, down my fingers and into the bowl. She continued to squeeze my hand until the last bit of juice left the lemon.

Satisfied, she smiled. At what, I couldn't say. She let go of my hand and shook hers toward the bowl so that drops of lemon juice flew into it. A few drops hit my hand that still hung suspended. I stared at the woman. I was dumbfounded for a few seconds, and she had to take the lemon from my hand and place it in the bowl. Once she did that, she made the sign of the cross over me and then the lemon juice.

She snapped her fingers in front of me a few times and said something. I had no idea what the woman said or why she had done the freaky lemon thing. I wiped my hand on a blanket and lay down to go back to sleep, but she wouldn't let me. She pestered me with foreign words until I got up and followed her to the bathroom, where she pointed to the shower.

"Lady, it's the middle of the night; can't I just take one in the morning?"

She half-smiled and pointed to a clock on the wall: Six o'clock in the morning. Forget that. I walked past her to the bed and flopped down. I needed at least three, maybe four, more hours of sleep. The moment my body hit the bed she began slapping my leg.

"Okay! Okay! Stop," I said. I fought not to groan, but instead muttered, "Goddamn it."

Her head whipped around so quickly that I threw my hands up. "Okay, sorry. Won't happen again."

She gave me one last, cold stare before snapping her fingers and pointing down the hallway. I hurried down. *Don't say God's name in vain.* Got it.

Having not showered for days, I had hoped for a long hot shower—but not in Laredo. My grandmother flushed the toilet after I had been in the shower five minutes? The hot water turned icy cold, and my hollering mixed with her laughter.

After the shower, my grandmother made sure I didn't fall back asleep by checking on me every few minutes. When she was satisfied that I appeared decent, she beckoned me to follow her down the hall. There were two other doors in the hallway besides the bathroom, but both doors were closed, so I couldn't see inside. Our destination was the yellow kitchen. My grandmother had turned the lights on since darkness still reigned outside. My eyes burned.

She said something I didn't understand and pointed to the table, where breakfast had been laid out. I sat down, instantly ravenous, since I hadn't eaten dinner the night before. In the background, my grandmother rummaged in the cabinets.

Breakfast consisted of a plate of scrambled eggs and a tortilla. I hated scrambled eggs—fried was the only way I ate them. I picked up the fork next to the plate and moved the eggs around, debating whether I should eat them or ask her to make me some the way I liked them. After a few minutes, the banging ceased in the kitchen. I looked up to find my grandmother glaring at me with a towel held against her hip. Over her wide body she wore a white apron that had red flowers stitched around the edges. Her lips pursed and her tiny eyes narrowed sharply at me.

"I don't like scrambled eggs."

"*Come.*" She pointed to the plate. *Co-may?*

"I don't know what you're saying, but could you just fry me some eggs instead?"

"*¡Come!* Eat now."

"Thought you couldn't speak English," I muttered beneath my breath.

I stabbed a few pieces of egg, a little more forcefully than needed, and placed them in my mouth. Cold eggs. Great. My mother had just abandoned me—one fried egg wasn't a crazy request. My grandmother watched me until I swallowed. When she was satisfied I would eat, she turned around and started muttering to herself as she did whatever it was she had been doing before.

I ate my breakfast in silence, while my grandmother prepared something. At least "something" is the only way I could describe it. Bowls and jars filled at various levels with powders, spices and other tiny things I didn't recognize sat on the counter. Every once in a while she poured different items into a boiling pot on the stove.

Other times, she threw in spices and a few times she even went to the plants by the door, tore some leaves off and threw them into the mix. Gradually, a horrible smell began to permeate the room. The words "rotting flesh" came to mind. It didn't take long for the smell to become so pungent that I had to put down the cold tortilla I had just taken a bite from and breathe slowly through my mouth to keep from heaving up the eggs I had just finished. I decided to go to the bathroom at the same time the front door opened.

"María!" a shrill voice rang through the house. More words followed, filled with the changing of excited tones.

I sprang out of my seat to leave the kitchen. I didn't want to meet anyone, especially not another Spanish-speaker. Unfortunately, my grandmother turned to me, pointed a knife she had been holding and said something that I imagined meant, "Move and I cut you." I sat without thinking. *Respect God and sharp pointy objects.* We were really getting to know each other.

Seconds later, a short woman with thin folds of skin hanging from her neck carried a large burlap sack into the kitchen, never ceasing her chatter. My grandmother wiped the knife on her apron, put her hand on her hip and waited. The woman appeared the same age as my grandmother. Her skin, wrinkled and stretched, hung on her wiry frame, and her roots had a grayish tint. The woman spied me and her words stopped mid-sentence. Her thin, wrinkled lips pursed together and she looked at my grandmother, then at me. She nodded her head a few times, crossed her arms and then said something in Spanish.

A quick burst of laughter escaped my grandmother's throat. "No, no, no." She shook both her hands in front of her, to emphasize the "nos."

The woman's eyes narrowed at my grandmother. She walked to the table and put her bag down before turning to me with a smile. I struggled not to tell her that her lipstick had smudged onto the skin above her top lip.

The woman spoke. I caught the name Gloria, but that was it. She grabbed my hand and, without warning, bent over and kissed me on my cheek! No one had ever kissed me. I couldn't even remember the last time *my mother* had kissed me.

When she pulled back, she placed her hands on my shoulders and waited for a response.

"Uh . . . " was all I could manage.

Her forehead creased and her black eyebrows narrowed together. Something about those small movements triggered something in my mind. It looked familiar. I wanted this woman away from me, as in five to ten paces. I looked to my grandmother, my face screaming for help. By now, she laughed so hard that tears rolled down her face. The woman looked over her shoulder and yelled something at my grandmother.

Through her tears and laughter, my grandmother strung a few words together. Something she said hit home for the woman still holding my shoulders, because her hands tightened on me and her body stiffened. Slowly her head turned towards me.

"¿Martha?" But instead of pronouncing the 'h' in my name, it sounded more like "Marta."

I nodded regardless.

I closed my eyes when the tiny woman grabbed me in a hug and kissed both of my cheeks this time. I opened my eyes in surprise when she put her hands on my face and spoke fast in Spanish. She pulled my face to her and gave me one last smack on my left cheek and then finally let

me go. She smiled wide with thin lips and straight white
teeth.

My body wanted to run but I couldn't. The woman's
smile faltered. She spoke a string of words and pointed
to herself with both her hands. Through the slur of
words, I picked out the name "Gloria," repeated over and
over.

Finally, my grandmother spoke up. One sentence,
simple and short.

Gloria didn't even turn around to look at my grandmother. Her lips pursed, and in a split second, a thought
came to my mind. A moment later, Gloria spoke, con-
firming my thoughts—well . . . kind of.

"What do you mean *my great niece* don't speak Spanish?"

For the next half hour, my grandmother and newly discovered aunt chattered and twittered in a language that
felt harsh to my ears and annoyed my whole being. I finally crossed my arms on the table and laid my forehead on
them, trying to tune out the words that flew around the
room. I considered sneaking in a nap, but their gibberish
prevented sleep from taking over my body.

As soon as my aunt had discovered my identity and
the fact that I couldn't speak Spanish, she quickly
switched to English to Spanish and began to hammer at
my grandmother. My grandmother cleaned my breakfast
dish and continued to brew her potion over the stove as
she replied with short answers and sometimes with that
backhanded flick of her wrist and a loud *"Pah!"* sound.

The noxious fumes assaulted my stomach, and I
prayed for the smell to disappear or to lose my sense of
smell altogether. Thirty minutes later, someone knocked

on the door. Another visitor? I had to stifle my groan. My grandmother picked up the boiling pot with two potholders and shuffled out of the kitchen. She called out something over her shoulder and walked into the hallway. My aunt responded, and with a narrowing of her eyes in my direction, she left the kitchen to answer the door.

Gloria greeted someone in the living room. My aunt walked in first, followed by a tall, dark, chestnut-colored woman holding a plastic garbage sack that bulged and stretched with its items. My aunt said something to the woman in Spanish and motioned to me.

"She don't speak Spanish. Can you believe it?" Gloria said, then turned her attention to me. "Martha, this is Doña Lorena."

What an odd name.

Doña Lorena had a frown on her very large lips. Her expression said she pitied my lack of Spanish. She had on a white dress with lace trimmings that hung loosely on her small upper body. Her hips were so wide that she looked like a bloated pear in a white-laced napkin. I couldn't bring myself to speak, so I just nodded once. Doña Lorena nodded back and then turned to Gloria.

"Where should I put this?"

Gloria pointed to the side of the kitchen, against the wall. As Doña Lorena went to set the black trash bag down, a six-year-old boy walked in. Walked isn't exactly the right word. He limped into the kitchen, but it had to be the oddest limp I had ever seen because he limped on both feet, which were encased in brown, dirt-caked sandals. He moved slowly, walking on the heels of his feet. His face was strained and he bit down on his lower lip as he struggled to walk.

"Oh, *m'ijo*." Doña Lorena stood up and looked at the boy.

I knew he was her son from the tone of her voice.

Gloria took her chair and dragged it over to the boy so he didn't have to walk any further. *"Pobrecito,"* she cooed.

The boy took even longer to sit down in the chair. Once he did, he wiped at his eyes. All my thoughts of what my mother did left for the moment. My hands became restless in my lap so that I had to clasp them together to keep from reaching out. I wanted to help him, but what could I do that his mother couldn't?

The little boy's body sagged as if he had just run a marathon rather than walked into the kitchen, and perhaps it was the same. Gloria and Doña Lorena started a conversation in Spanish. Doña Lorena couldn't have been family. I figured Gloria would have let me know by then. If she wasn't family, why were they here? Gloria fetched a glass of water for the boy. He accepted it with a murmur.

The boy had shiny, black hair cut straight across his forehead, and his heart-shaped face resembled his mother's. He had the same dark brown skin, too, but unlike his mother, he was skinny. His thin and faded shirt complimented his jeans that had a hole over the right knee. He sipped his water, and as he did, he noticed me. It must have been the first time he realized someone besides Gloria was there. I smiled, which caused him to blush and look down at his cup. It was cute.

Seconds later, the squeaking of the floorboards warned of my grandmother's slow approach from the hallway. When she arrived, Gloria and Doña Lorena's conversation stopped. Doña Lorena moved to my grandmother and spoke to her. She pointed to the sack that lay against the wall, and as she spoke, my grandmother nodded every few seconds. My grandmother didn't have the stern look she had given me or Gloria a few times, but rather her features had softened to an understanding, concerned look. She walked over to the young boy and bent over, resting her hands on her knees.

She spoke to him and he smiled. She stood back up and he handed the glass of water to Gloria. He took a deep breath, bit his lip and stood up carefully, wincing as his feet touched the floor. He walked oddly as he had before, following my grandmother out of the kitchen and into the hallway. The slow procession ended with Doña Lorena, shoulders slumped, following at a slow pace. Gloria and I were left alone in a claustrophobic silence, interrupted a few seconds later by the sound of a door closing down the hallway.

Gloria walked over to the backyard door, pushed aside a few potted plants with her foot and then opened it. She pulled a cigarette and lighter out of her pocket, stood by the door and began to smoke. I hated smoke and how it burnt the canals of my nostrils. My mother used to smoke sometimes at night in our apartment, and each time I'd go to my room and get under the covers to escape the acrid odor. There were times when my "room" was the couch, and then, there was no escaping. Thinking about my mother made my stomach churn.

Gloria broke the silence. "I can't believe you don't speak no Spanish."

I shrugged in response.

"Don't tell your grandmother I'm smoking, 'kay?"

"Why?"

"Because I'm your *tía*." As if there would be any other reason.

"What's tee-ya?"

"Tía. Not tee-yuh," she said emphasizing the 'yuh.' "Your aunt." She shook her head as she blew out the smoke.

"I'm bored."

"Of course you are. Sorry that Laredo isn't New York or all the fancy places you've been."

"I've never been to New York. My mother and I were in Memphis last. Not really what you'd call fancy."

She shook her head. "Your mother . . . that girl!"

I snorted. "Yeah."

Gloria looked at me sideways. "She always caused headaches."

"You're telling me."

"Hey! Watch your mouth. That's your mother."

"But you just said . . . "

She flicked a few ashes off her cigarette. "I know what I said. But that don't mean you disrespect her."

I looked away and rolled my eyes. Adults.

We sat there for a few minutes, Gloria smoking and me bored out of my mind.

"So how come you speak English and she doesn't?" I asked.

Gloria blew out a puff of smoke. "I worked in the cafeteria at the Air Force Base for twenty years. Had to learn *para los gringos*."

I gave her a blank stare. Why did she keep using Spanish?

She rolled her eyes, "White people, Martha. *Híjole*."

After a few seconds, Gloria asked, "Your mamá didn't tell you about me?"

"Nope."

Her eyes hardened. She shook her head back and forth as she muttered things in Spanish. Once she stopped, I laid my head back on my arms and relaxed. Maybe I could get a nap. Unexpectedly, a shriek cut through the house.

"What the hell?"

Gloria put out her cigarette on the door frame and pointed it at me. "Watch your mouth, *muchacha!*"

"What's going on back there?"

Gloria closed the door and walked back to the table. She sat down and threw the cigarette in her bag as she answered me. "What you mean? She's healing him."

"Healing him of what? Why is he screaming?"

"From *el Diablo*. Didn't you see how he walked in here? She has to purge *el Diablo* from his *pies.*"

"What? Speak English."

She slapped her open palm on the table. "Ah, *tu* mamá teach you nothing! The Devil! The Devil has poisoned the boy's feet. Large sores cover his feet and threaten his life. *Tu* abuela is cleansing him of the disease. Why do you think she made that awful stuff?"

"Wait, so my grandmother is a doctor?"

Gloria had begun to lean back in her chair when she abruptly popped forward at my question. "What? Your mother didn't tell you?" She turned her head, studying me with one open eye while the other squinted.

"Tell me what?"

"*¡Ay, Dios mío!*" She put her hand to her forehead and pushed her hair back. "*M'ija, tu abuela,* she's a *curandera.*" Her voice changed as she said *curandera*. It dripped in awe of the word and whatever it meant.

"*Tee-yuh,*" I pronounced each syllable, "what is a cur-cur-dra?"

"*¡Curandera!*" Her lips and tongue pronounced the word with such intensity and purpose that I flinched. "A *curandera* is a healer. They are better than doctors. They can cure anything with the power of God. Your *abuela, mi hermana,*" she thumped her chest for effect, "is the best of them all! Not like these *charlatanes con* their stores on Saunders and McPherson."

"Are *charla—ta—*, whatever you just said, is different than what my grandmother is?"

Gloria slapped her forehead. "*Ay, n'ombre.* You know nothing. No, *charlatanes,* you know, charlatans in *inglés*? They are people around town claiming they have the gift to heal, opening stores in Laredo, selling fake charms, doing healings, all the while stealing good people's money! Giving my sister a bad name." She began to shake her head back and forth in anger.

Thousands of questions hit me at once, and I couldn't choose which one to ask first. Gloria stood up and began rummaging in one of the cabinets, looking for something, as if the news she had just laid on me should be accepted so easily.

"So what is she doing with that stuff she made? Making him drink it, or what?"

"How would I know? Do I look like a curandera to you?"

I had to bite my tongue from saying that I didn't understand what a curandera was, much less what they looked like.

Gloria pulled a small, ten-inch, yellow television from a cabinet, placed it on the counter and plugged the cord into a socket on the wall. She moved the antennae around a bit and then opened a drawer and pulled out a brown remote.

"How do you know it's the Devil hurting the boy? What if he just has an infection?"

Gloria pressed a button and the television sprang to life. Of course, the station was all in Spanish.

"You ask too many questions. Now, *silencio, las novelas* are on."

I leaned back in my chair and let out a huge huff. Gloria's attention focused solely on the whispered dialog of what looked like a soap opera.

For the next half hour my mind reeled. Gloria, too involved with her TV show, never gave me a second look. What did my grandmother do in the back room? Did the weird lemon thing she made me do that morning have to do with being a healer? Was my grandmother some voodoo witch or crazy, religious exorcist? After a while, I debated whether or not to go to the bathroom to spy on my grandmother, but as soon as I thought it, a door creaked open in the back.

I sat up, waiting for them to enter the kitchen. Gloria muttered something under her breath. She grabbed the remote and turned off the television, then looked down the hallway. Doña Lorena entered the kitchen with a small smile on her lips. She had to turn sideways so her wide hips could fit through the doorway. My grandmother followed, and finally the boy walked in. He limped but not as severely as before. His face didn't strain as much and he didn't bite his lips. Off-white bandages had been wrapped around his feet, and the lingering scent of the awful-smelling potion filled the room when he entered.

He smiled at me before dropping his head in shyness. I returned the smile. My grandmother must have helped him in some way. He looked better. Gloria spoke to his mother as my grandmother went to the trash bag that

Doña Lorena had left in the kitchen earlier. She hauled it up and reached in, moving the contents around the bag until finally she pulled out something blue. It looked like a dress that could fit my grandmother.

Doña Lorena excused herself from Gloria and asked my grandmother something. My grandmother nodded and pointed toward me. Doña Lorena studied me from top to bottom and responded back. What was that about?

She grabbed my grandmother's hands once my grandmother had set the bag down, all the while speaking in Spanish. Doña Lorena turned and spoke to her son, who in turn spoke to my grandmother. His voice barely rose above a whisper, as if he couldn't help being shy. My grandmother's face softened and she kissed the top of his head.

I envied the boy right then: kindness from a stranger, my own grandmother; he had a mother who loved him, who would never leave him behind at a relative's house; a mother who kept him safe, who wanted him to be healed.

I felt a burn in my throat, but I choked it down.

Moments later, the mother and son left, and we were alone again in the house. My grandmother ignored Gloria and me and returned to the back room.

"Gloria, can I go to my room?"

"No, stay right there."

"Why?"

"Because your *abuela* said so."

For the next two hours, I sat in the kitchen as more visitors came to call: old men, young women, young couples, large women, ugly men, beautiful women and even a very old lady who wore an orange hat. The only thing that they had in common was the brown color of their skin and the language they spoke. Sometimes they would go to the back with my grandmother, but mostly she would come to the kitchen and give them a small pouch or object. They'd hold it close to their breast as if to hide it from my prying eyes.

Some of the guests brought things, like Doña Lorena had. One old man brought a bowl of tan eggs. A young girl, probably only a few years older than me, handed my grandmother hand-painted plates of Jesus and Mary—as if she didn't have a billion already. Most of the time my grandmother would hand the gift back and shake her head no, but everyone pushed their gifts back into her hands and wouldn't take no for an answer.

And they all looked at me, wondering who I was and why I stared at them. The bold ones asked Gloria or my grandmother who I was by nodding toward me or motioning with their hand. Most just acknowledged me with a nod or a smile when they discovered that I didn't understand them. Luckily, no one attacked me with kisses, although one wrinkled man considered it, leaving me instead with a creepy wink and the smacking sound of toothless gums.

I was bored the entire morning. When Gloria finished watching her television shows, she turned a radio on to a Mexican music station. After a bit, I asked her if we could change it.

"To what?" she said.

"Something that plays rock. You know, Nirvana, AC/DC, Pearl Jam?"

She crossed herself. "Rock music? ¡Mierda! Don't bring that devil music in here."

So I was subjected to long hours of music that I didn't understand and didn't like.

Finally, I was able to convince Gloria to let me run to
my room and grab an old journal with some empty
pages and a pencil. I passed most of the time drawing
the kitchen and the little boy from that morning. Gloria
watched me suspiciously and every once in a while she
leaned over and looked at my drawings. She never made
a comment, only said, "Hmm," which was probably the
only bit of praise that I would ever get from her.

After a long morning, my grandmother came to the
kitchen and prepared us lunch—tortillas and some of the
rice stuff from the night before. After a few moments of
staring at it, smelling it, examining it from every angle,
and after the pointed stares from my grandmother and
Gloria, I finally took a bite. Rather bland, it could have
used some salt. But the tortillas were warm and the
chicken didn't taste half bad. I wasn't all that hungry,
though, so I left quite a bit on my plate. That was until
Gloria told me to eat it all, that little children across the
river were starving. I didn't know what she was talking
about, but my grandmother held a butter knife in her
hand and it looked like she considered using it on me if
I didn't eat. I forced the rest down.

Not even a full day and I had already been threat-
ened twice with knives. Welcome to Laredo.

After lunch, Gloria left and my grandmother and I
were alone together in a house that shrunk with every
breath. Once she had washed the dishes, my grandmother pointed at my feet and then to her shoes. It didn't take
a rocket scientist to understand that she wanted me to
put some shoes on. I trudged down the hall and grabbed
my sandals. I wanted to try one of the doors to see what
my grandmother had been doing with all her "patients,"

but I feared she'd hear the creaking hinges. When I returned, she looked at the sandals I wore and chuckled.

"What?"

She went to my room and pointed to a pair of tennis shoes in my suitcase.

I shook my head no and pointed to my sandals. I'm not sure why. I just didn't like this woman telling me to do things. My mother never told me to do anything. And anyway, who did she think she was, dictating what kind of shoes I wore?

She shrugged and walked past me, grinning, into the hallway.

We left the house only to be bombarded by the sweltering heat wave of the summer. My grandmother walked the street towards the gold car, but instead of getting in, she turned right and walked past it. I hesitated and then followed her, disappointed that we weren't going to drive the car to our destination. And then a worse thought hit me: we were actually going to walk through the neighborhood. I kept close to her, not that it would have helped. My grandmother had to be seventy or eighty. What could she do to those scary Mexican guys I had seen the day before?

We walked on the right side of the street, since there weren't any sidewalks. My sandals slapped against the pavement and echoed through the hollow neighborhood. There weren't that many people out at the moment. Perhaps they were at work? A few old people sat on their porches staring at us when we walked by. We also passed a few ladies who chatted vigorously with one another. They called out to my grandmother in Spanish and waved. She just smiled and nodded.

The houses blurred as we walked by. I focused only on the back of my grandmother's head as I walked behind her. I stopped focusing on everything around us and began to notice something else. My sandals had become unbearably hot, and they were becoming hotter by the minute. My feet started burning as if I had placed them over a blazing bonfire.

"Holy crap!" I ran to one of the yards, unfortunately without any grass, and pulled my sandals off, but as soon as my feet touched the dirt lawn, they began to burn again. The lawn wasn't as hot as the street, but it still seared the soles of my feet. If the street was a bonfire, the dirt ground was an oven set on high. Through the scorching pain on the bottoms of my feet and the incessant *ouches* and *ows* that burst from my mouth, I heard my grandmother laughing. I looked up as I hopped from foot to foot.

My grandmother was bent at the waist with her hands on her knees laughing. She stood up and said, "*Ajá, tonta.*" She pointed at me and chuckled a few times, ignoring my pain. Between laughs she said something else I didn't understand. Finally, her laughter died down and she said, "Okay, *vamos, tonta.*" She motioned with her head for me to follow her.

I made a frustrated noise in my throat. "You knew this would happen! You let me come out here with sandals on and you knew this would happen!"

She flipped her hand and wrist backward, and said, "*Vamos, tonta.*"

I put my sandals back on my feet. What else could I do? My grandmother began to walk, expecting me to follow, but I would not walk behind her like a poodle on a leash. For the next three miles, I trudged through the yellow and brown yards, making my way into the street whenever a chained dog barked or someone sat out on their front lawn.

By the time we reached our destination, my feet were beyond repair. The straps had rubbed the skin raw on the top of my feet, creating a sea of blisters. The skin on the bottom of my feet had been stripped away so that I suffered a non-stop scalding sensation with every step I took. I walked on the inner arches of my feet like a pigeon-toed dog with thorns in its paws. I gritted my teeth and forced the hisses and moans down my throat. I would not give my grandmother the satisfaction of hearing my pain.

I'd have walked a thousand more miles until my feet broke off at the ankles, if only our destination had turned out differently. When I spied the red brick building splayed across a mile of deadened yellow grass, the star spangled banner waving high on a flag pole, and the large sign that said, "Go Conquistadors!" in peeling letters, the pain in my feet let up some as panic swept throughout my body.

I stopped in my tracks. "You're enrolling me in *this* school?"

My grandmother's steps didn't falter as she trudged up the path toward the front doors.

Her laughter floated on the air, wrapping me in its mockery.

Tres

AS SOON AS MY GRANDMOTHER and the principal exited his office, I knew she had been successful in enrolling me in school. The principal's face was pale, the color of the white apron my grandmother wore to cook in. I fumed the entire way back to the house.

How did my grandmother do it? I couldn't imagine that my mother left my important paperwork behind before she hopped out of the window and sped off in her car. It had to be against the law to let someone into school without the proper documents, right? Perhaps my grandmother used some voodoo witch power of hers to convince him? Or a threat! He did look frightened when we left. And there hadn't been anyone else in the office to save me or the principal from this cursed enrollment. Had she called him to meet us there? And when?

When we arrived at the house, I limped to my bedroom, fully understanding the pain of the boy with the disease in his feet. I had just fallen onto the bed when I heard my grandmother shuffle into the room. She grabbed my foot. I almost cried out in pain, but she began to massage something soothing onto my foot, and the pain faded away.

I sat up. She had pulled a stool up to the bed and was rubbing a brown paste from a jar onto my right foot. Her hands moved along the contours, kneading the paste into the blisters and sores. For a moment, the word "infection" crossed my mind, but the thought vanished quickly. The pain in my foot eased away with each press of her finger. After a few seconds, the pain was mostly gone. How could it disappear so quickly? When she finished with my right foot, she worked on the left.

Minutes later, she screwed the lid back on the jar before placing it on the table next to the candles.

I murmured, "Thank you," when she stood up.

She looked down at me and gave a slight nod. We had crossed an invisible line, and neither one of us knew what to do about it. My grandmother made the next move. She went to my suitcase and pulled out a ratty pair of tennis shoes that was covered in layers of brown dirt. She spoke, pointing at the shoes.

"We're leaving again? Can I just stay here, please?"

She tossed the shoes at me. They almost hit me in the face. So much for that invisible line.

For two hours that Saturday, we walked from house to house through the labyrinth of neighborhoods. Most of the time, we handed whoever answered the door a jar or pouch from her large bag. My grandmother spoke with them and then we left. Sometimes we went into the houses, where my grandmother disappeared down the halls, and I waited in a living room or kitchen alone or with someone until she finished. I never spoke to anyone, and no one spoke to me. I assumed my grandmother told them that I didn't speak Spanish.

After two grueling hours, we walked down a street where the houses thinned out until finally only businesses lined both sides. At the end, we rounded a corner into a bustling market area. Carts, booths and stores

lined the streets, and men, women and children walked
between them. I smelled a mixture of things: cooking
meat, sweet pastries and the sweat from a crowd of people baking in the hot air.

We walked through the market, looking at this booth
and that. Everyone knew my grandmother. We hadn't
even made it to our first booth, when a man ran up to us
with two large Dixie cups filled with a red juice that had
oranges and other colorful fruit floating in it. I gulped it
down as he and my grandmother spoke. Others came up
to us from time to time with smiles and handshakes and
even a few hugs for my grandmother. My grandmother
got items from many booths, but I never saw her
exchange money with anyone. The owners scrambled to
give her their tortillas, their drinks, their oranges, their
bags of sugar—all for free.

The day passed by in a whirlwind. If the whirlwind
had a sound, it would have been the rapid tones of Spanish blowing me off balance with each syllable. But
strangely enough, by the end of the day, I did have a
sense of Spanish. I could tell when someone pleaded or
showered my grandmother in thanks. Most of all, I knew
when someone spoke about me. Perhaps I only picked
up on their body language or the tone of the language,
but that's more than I had been able to do the day before,
and it surprised me.

By the time we made it to a clothing shop, the last stop
of the day, my arms ached with the weight of our buys
and my feet ached within my tennis shoes. Doña Lorena
greeted us at the door with a long plastic bag, from which
peeked a few hangers. The two talked and then my grandmother took the bag and draped it over her arm. We left
soon and made the long trip back to her house.

That night we had something called *mole*. I wasn't even hungry after a full day of walking. The bed called to my aching, tired body, but my grandmother refused to allow me to sleep without eating. Mole ended up being lumps of chicken meat under a spicy, yet somewhat sweet, chocolate-tasting sauce. I could only stomach a few pieces on my own, but I force-fed myself the rest because my grandmother would not stop repeating, "*¡Come! ¡Come!*" every few minutes. After dinner, I went straight to my room and fell into a deep sleep.

The next day, God slapped me in the face.

I woke up to my grandmother speaking Spanish to me. She bustled about grabbing the clothes I had left on the floor. When I wiped the sleep from my eyes and pushed myself up onto my elbow, she pointed at me and then at the plastic bag we had picked up from Doña Lorena that hung on the door.

"Okay, okay," I said, anything to shut her up. I'd look at whatever she wanted me to look at after I showered.

Ten minutes later, I took the bag down from the hook on the door. "No way. There's no way," I said.

My grandmother must have heard me because she came down the hallway. She started pointing and shaking her finger at me as soon as she saw me in my underwear and bra. That was the least of her problems. She started pointing at the clothes I'd dropped onto the floor and then at me.

"Why do you want me to wear this?"

"*Para la iglesia.*"

"What?"

She threw her hands in the air in frustration, then pointed to the large Jesus on the wall.

"For Jesus?"

She shook her head at me. *"Iglesia. Iglesia."* She put her forefingers together so they pointed upward.

What was she . . . wait . . . a steeple? "Church? We're going to church?" I shook my head no.

"Sí, sí."

I let out a groan. "Okay, but if I'm going, I'm not wearing that!"

My grandmother crossed her arms and gave me a cold stare. I crossed my arms and stared back. We stood there for what seemed like hours, until I looked away. The intensity behind my grandmother's eyes burned through me until I couldn't hold it any longer.

She smiled at my defeat, turned around and walked down the hallway. I made a frustrated noise and stomped my foot. Childish, but considering what I had to wear, it made sense.

It was a canary yellow dress made out of lace and silk. When I slung it on, it hung loosely on my thin frame. It had yellow ruffles on the sleeves and a yellow bow that tied around my waist and fell limply in front. It hugged my neck, choking me like a boa constrictor hiding all of my dirty bits from God and Heaven above. The ensemble even came with white panty hose and matching white sandals. My short, brown hair looked dingy against the yellow collar. A slight wave had formed on the right side of my head and no matter how much I brushed it, it wouldn't go straight. I huffed at the mirror.

I looked like a school-girl-gone-bad. I was sixteen years old! The dress looked like something a freaking five-year-old would wear. Did I mention the white sandals? They pinched the sides of my feet. If my mother saw me now . . . she'd die. Did my mother stand here once in a similar dress her mother had made her wear? Is that why she left?

My grandmother smiled when she saw me and smoothed out a wrinkle on the front of the dress. I fought not to vomit. We took the gold Cadillac and picked up Gloria on our way.

St. Augustine's was a tan-colored building with dark gray roofing and one steeple attached to the back of a longer building. What looked like a two-story house with Roman columns had been placed at the front of the church. It was a plain church, besides the columns and steeple, but better kept than the tired area in which it was set.

The polished, wooden doors stood wide open and were taller than the height of two men. People flocked toward its doors, speaking rapidly to one another. Every other girl my age wore something horribly similar to what I did, which made me feel less like a freak. I have to admit, the boys had it worse. They wore long sleeve shirts and pants. Some even had on suits and ties, despite the hundred-degree temperature.

Just like in the market, people greeted my grandmother and Gloria as if they were queens. I stood by their side, miserable already, and we weren't even in the church yet. When we did make it inside, I almost stumbled. The ceiling stretched high, with bright lights shining down on us. Statues of Mary, Jesus and his disciples lined the walls between the glass mosaics that depicted saints doing various deeds, like healing the sick or praying on a hill.

The pews were filled, and for a moment, happiness filled me at the idea of having to leave. But my grandmother dipped her hand in a bowl of water next to the door, made the sign of the cross over her body and trudged forward. Gloria followed. I looked at the bowl for a moment and then followed Gloria up the middle aisle.

About halfway down, a bad feeling creeped up my neck until I cringed. The feeling of someone's eyes on my back made me turn around and look over my shoulder. It didn't take long to figure out whose eyes were trained on me. Sitting at the edge of the aisle, on the left, was the girl that had left my grandmother's house a few days ago. The same girl from my dream. I almost didn't recognize her with her hair down and curled instead of pulled back in a slick bun. She wore a black taffeta dress that covered her arms and fell to the floor. Her eyes, though, were recognizable by the black fire that filled their depths. Thick, black eyeliner and blacker mascara just added a more chilling effect.

I pulled at the neckline of my dress, hot all of a sudden. Who was the girl? And why did she hate me? Because it was obvious she did. She'd only seen me twice now, and her hatred could be read on every feature of her face. I walked a little faster and caught up with my grandmother and Gloria, wanting to be as far from the girl as possible.

We finally came to the third row from the front, where, amazingly, a space for three had been spared at the end of the aisle. My grandmother kneeled, making the sign of the cross over her chest. Gloria did the same. I bent my head and sat down. My grandmother and Gloria were on their knees on a bench that folded out from the pew in front of us, their hands folded in prayer. My grandmother looked at me and frowned. She turned to Gloria and whispered something to her. Gloria's head whipped toward me.

"What are you doing?" she whispered.

"Nothing," I whispered back.

She frowned. "I see that. Why aren't you praying?"

"I've never been to church. I don't know what to do."

She clutched her chest and opened her mouth in shock. Her eyes bugged out, and for a moment it looked as if she would suffer a heart attack.

"Never. Been. To church?!"

I couldn't tell if it was a statement or a question, so I remained silent under her accusing eyes. She shook her head and then made a quick sign of the cross. She closed her eyes and pressed her hands tightly in prayer. Her lips moved but no words came out. She probably prayed for my salvation from Eternal Hell. My grandmother stared at me with lips pursed. She looked to the altar and began praying again.

Church consisted mostly of watching a graying priest in gold and green robes walking around the altar and giving a sermon in Spanish. I worked hard not to fall asleep to his monotone voice. I woke only to the unexpected movements of the entire church. Everybody else was privy to an invisible signal that alerted them to sit, stand and kneel at different points of the service. The first time it occurred, I remained seated until Gloria turned to me with a fiery glare and told me to stand up. From then on, I sat, stood and kneeled a second behind everyone else. By the end of the service, my back and knees ached.

At one point, everyone filed into line and the guy in the robe placed something in their mouths and then gave them something to drink out of a gold goblet. My grandmother made me go to the front and cross my arms in an "X" over my chest. It took forever for me to understand what she wanted me to do. The line halted for two minutes, as she crossed her arms and nodded her head at me, whispering at me in Spanish in hopes that I would understand.

"I don't understand," I whispered back.

Finally, Gloria quickly intervened and told me what to do. The man in the robes, who looked pretty annoyed by the delay, made the sign of the cross over me and spoke some words. The only other people I saw this also happen to were little children. I hated that I didn't know what anything meant, as if I wasn't lost enough here in the new world that I had been dumped into.

An hour and thirty minutes later my boredom ended. I think I walked faster to the car than Gloria or my grandmother did. For the first time since I'd been abandoned, a smile formed on my lips at the thought of returning to the pink shack. Fifteen minutes later, we pulled up to a sea-green house with white trim. Battered trucks and worn-down cars littered the front yard and the driveway. A spot just wide enough for the Cadillac had been conveniently saved directly in front of the house.

"Where are we?"

Gloria turned around and looked at me. "We are at your tía Juanita's."

"Your sister?"

She raised her eyebrow and looked at my grandmother, who ignored her and got out of the car.

"Your *madre* tell you nothing? Juanita is your mother's sister." She got out of the car without waiting to see my reaction.

My mother has a sister? A mom, an aunt and now a sister. Did my mother have another child somewhere that she forgot to mention, too? Any other important person she had kept me away from? My father maybe?

I set my mouth in a firm line, refusing to let the lump forming at the base of my throat to rise. I opened the car door so I could meet another freaking aunt.

Gloria and my grandmother were already inside the house by the time I made it up the steps and to the door. I reached out for the handle and hesitated. I was going to meet my aunt, my mother's *sister*. Would she know why my mother had left me? Or even why she left Laredo in the first place and never told me about our family? Perhaps my mother had stopped by here on her way out of the city. Maybe she was still in the city and, if not, well, this aunt might know where my mother was. I needed these answers. I opened the door.

A mixture of noise hit my ears as soon as I opened the door. The sweet and spicy vapors of food hit my nose and created a warmth deep inside my stomach. My mouth started watering for food that I probably wouldn't recognize or even be able to pronounce. Words and laughter floated from other rooms, words I didn't understand and laughter that I wished for.

At the end of the entryway my grandmother and Gloria were talking to a few people and apparently had forgotten about me. To my left stood a small table filled with pictures. It didn't take long to figure out who my aunt was. She had long, straight, black hair and the same small, button nose that my mother had. My aunt's face was longer and narrower, like Gloria's, but she had my grandmother's small thin lips. Children filled the pictures as did a man, whom I assumed was her husband. I came to the last picture and stopped short.

My hand reached out for the frame and I pulled it closer for a better look. The maroon frame held an old black-and-white picture of two girls standing in front of a white truck. One girl, older and taller than the other, appeared about eight years of age, and the other looked about six years old. They both had their arms around each other's shoulders, smiling with matching toothless gaps at the camera. I rubbed my thumb over the figure of the older girl—my mother.

Despite her young age, the contours of her face peeked through the youthful chubbiness of her cheeks. The other girl was my aunt. I stared at the picture willing some kind of feeling to rise up. My mother looked happy with her sister.

A feminine voice rang out in Spanish behind me. Startled, I hurriedly placed the frame down and turned around.

A young woman, a few inches shorter than me, stood smiling. She wore her Sunday best, a purple blouse and a matching flowery skirt, with her hair pulled back in a French braid. I would soon learn that this was my aunt Juanita.

"She didn't tell you, either?" Gloria asked my aunt.

The woman's smile faltered as she turned to look at Gloria and my grandmother. The people who had been speaking with them had left, leaving us four women in the hallway together.

"Tell me what? Mamá, ¿quién es ella?" Aunt Juanita said.

My grandmother looked at me and then at Aunt Juanita, her lips set firmly and a tiredness forming around her eyes. She sighed, turned around and headed through a doorway, shaking her head. Gloria, hand on her hip and a smirk on her face, appeared more than happy to relate the news of my identity.

"Juanita say, '*hola*,' to your niece, Martha. Rosa's daughter."

The woman's head snapped back to me the same time Gloria walked away. Juanita's wide eyes looked me over and within a few seconds she had studied every part of me. Her lips trembled and her mouth opened slightly.

"Rosa?" she said as she turned and looked for someone to come through the front door.

Guess my mother hadn't stopped by here on her way out of town.

"She's not here."

Aunt Juanita reminded me of a young girl, scared but hopeful. She didn't even press further, just said, "Oh."

I fidgeted, uncomfortable under her lost look, but she didn't seem to really see me. Her eyes looked at something distant in time. After a few moments, she returned to the present, shaking her head.

She cleared her throat, then said, "Hi, I'm Juanita."

"Martha."

"Nice to meet you," she said.

I nodded.

Awkward silence. I stood quiet, too shy to break it.

"So, Martha, how old are you?"

"Sixteen."

"Oh," she pondered this. "You're, uh, very tall for your age."

"Yeah."

She nodded her head as she smoothed out her skirt. "Well, let's introduce you to everyone." She smiled wide and genuinely, unlike my mother, and gestured at the doorway that my grandmother and Gloria had disappeared through.

I hesitated for a second, scared of what or who I would find through there. I took a step, and then another. Juanita followed behind me. Through the doorway, a number of brown faces and bodies pressed together in a living room, involved in loud and animated conversations with one another. Dark-haired children ran around in their miniature versions of suits and dresses. My grandmother and Gloria were nowhere in sight.

Juanita's hands placed themselves on my upper arms tentatively, a sign of comfort. No one noticed us at first. Juanita whistled a loud note and all the voices stopped at once. Every pair of brown and black eyes turned to us. Even the children stopped and turned to attention. A few heads popped out of a doorway across the room.

"*¡Familia! Ésta es la hija de Rosa . . . Martha. ¡Vamos a darle la bienvenida a Martha!*" The words sounded friendly, but that was all that I picked up.

My body tensed. Mouths dropped and bodies stilled.

"What did you just say?" I whispered to Juanita, turning my head slightly to see her face.

A small line formed across her brow, confused at my question. "This is your family. I told them who you were."

"Family?" And with that one word, a hundred brown bodies came to life and converged on me with smiles and hugs.

My family. What felt like a hundred people turned out to be only about thirty or forty people crammed into a tight space. For the next couple of hours they passed me from person to person and welcomed me home, even though this wasn't my home. They showered me with cheek kisses and large bear hugs. No personal space existed between us. One young woman with a baby on her hip pulled me into a one-armed hug and kissed the side of my face. The tallest and widest guy, who called himself "Tanque," pulled me into a big hug so that my face was squished into his belly and my arms were stuck to my sides.

It didn't take long for them to realize I didn't speak Spanish. Many switched to English or tried speaking English the best they could, but most were limited. I would have laughed at the way we tried to communicate if I hadn't been so disoriented and shocked. I kept an uncomfortable smile on my face and nodded or shook my head at most questions.

No one mentioned my mother or asked where she was, but only showered me with their attention, commenting on my height or asking how I liked Laredo. A few invited me to their houses or to future events. They encouraged me to get a plate of food, said how skinny I was and made disapproving faces at my thin figure. My grandmother and Gloria had helped to prepare the food in the kitchen while the family moved me about. Even the children tugged on my ugly, yellow dress, and with squeaky, accented voices, asked me to play. Juanita introduced me to her husband and her children, my cousins: a chubby, eight-year-old boy, Tomas, and a three-year-old girl named Lilia who had large, black ringlets and a big smile. She attached herself to me and called me *"prima,"* which Juanita said meant "cousin" in Spanish.

Everyone showered me with love and acceptance. Even so, I felt a growing pressure in my chest with each smiling face, each hug, each compliment or invitation to their home. After a while, I couldn't stand it any longer and finally asked someone to show me to the bathroom.

I stumbled into the bathroom, shut the door and dropped to the floor. The tears that I had been holding back for the last few hours broke free and my body rocked in sobs. A family. People who showered me with love the very first time they met me. She had denied me this. Denied me this love all these years. Ran from this place and kept me away from them. I had cousins, aunts, uncles, great aunts even. And she had never allowed me to be a part of this.

Juanita found me in there and knelt down beside me. She fidgeted, and then after a few moments she wrapped her arms around me and pulled me close. When the tears finally stopped, I pulled back, wiped them away with my arm and looked at her. She didn't look like my mother, didn't even wear make-up. Juanita had shown me more love in the last few minutes than my mother ever really had, but for some reason I couldn't stop thinking about my mother.

"So, you don't know where she is?"

Juanita shook her head. "I was going to ask you the same."

I laughed, and a few more tears escaped. "She just left me here and snuck out a window. I mean, who does that?"

Juanita's mouth opened and shut a few times trying to find the right words until she closed it without an answer.

"Do you know why she kept me away from all of this?"

"I have a good idea," she said.

I considered asking what she thought but I stopped. What did it matter? We sat quietly for a few moments.

"My mother might know where she's at," Juanita added.

"Will you ask her?"

The hope in my voice disgusted me. I had a family who welcomed me and still I wanted to leave. They didn't even know me—it wasn't like they'd miss me or anything. I couldn't live here with my grandmother and her stupid rules. I was doing fine before with a shitty mother. At least I did what I wanted. Most of all, I wanted to find her and tell her she was not allowed to abandon me like this. She was not freaking allowed to be the God-awful-piece-of-shit-mother that deep down I knew she was. And how the hell did my mother expect to take care of herself? She couldn't!

Juanita shook her head no. "If she knows, she won't tell me."

After a few seconds, the silence became awkward. "Well, you have a nice family," I said.

The spell broke. Her brown eyes turned to me, and she smiled. "*Nosotros tenemos una buena familia.*"

Then for my sake, she translated, "*We* have a good family."

An hour later, the sun set and the family left the house one by one, until Gloria, my grandmother and I were the only ones left with Juanita and her family. I played with Lilia while everyone cleaned up the house and the kitchen. I was exhausted. Too many faces and too many questions from strangers who acted as if we had known each other our whole lives. And then there had been Gloria running around telling everyone I didn't speak Spanish and, "Could you believe it? A Mexican who couldn't speak Spanish!" My grandmother sat there and watched me the entire time with a look of interest or maybe it was distaste. I couldn't figure out that lady and her moods.

We left soon after everything was cleaned up, took Gloria home and returned to the Pepto-Bismol house. Before I went down the hallway to my room, my grandmother stopped me. I waited in the kitchen as she went back into the living room. She returned with a brand new black backpack. She handed it to me and stood there awkwardly.

I unzipped it and found paper, pens, two spirals and a binder inside. I needed another spiral. The one I had was almost full. I zipped it back up. I had almost forgotten that tomorrow would be my first day of school in Laredo. A groan almost escaped my mouth at the thought of school, but my grandmother might have taken it the wrong way. Her gesture was nice. I had always had to buy my own second-hand backpacks from Goodwill or the Salvation Army and use them until a strap broke or the bottom seam ripped.

"Thanks."

She nodded her head once and said, *"De nada."*

Discomfort crept around us, so I moved to go to my room, but stopped and turned around. "Where's my mother?"

My grandmother's face didn't change. Her hard eyes searched mine, until I had to look away.

"No."

"No, you don't know where she is? Or, no, you're not going to tell me?"

"No," she repeated, before walking past me into the hallway.

Desperate, I asked, "Why did she leave me?"

Her retreating form never stopped to tell me. I stood holding the backpack as I heard a door close down the hall.

My grandmother wouldn't tell me. Then again, maybe she couldn't explain what I wanted to know because we couldn't understand each other. If that was the case, then that only left me with one more option: I needed to learn Spanish, become one of them, earn their trust and figure things out on my own.

Cuatro

MY FIRST-DAY-OF-SCHOOL OUTFIT consisted of a faded graphic T-shirt with the logo of a rock band from Memphis on the front, shorts and my white tennis shoes—I refused to stand out on my first day. My grandmother gave a narrowed look at my outfit before she rushed me to get my backpack. I should have been thankful she didn't make me wear another awful dress.

We headed out the door and into the early morning darkness. We took the same route as we had that Friday before, except this time instead of being the only ones on the street, we were among many teenagers going the same way, all of whom stared at us as we walked past. The entire walk, I kept my eyes focused on my grandmother's calloused heels that peeked out from her sandals.

When we arrived at the school, my grandmother headed straight to the front office. I didn't have time to study the groups of kids on the lawn, except to notice that every single student appeared Mexican. A first for a new school.

A girl with glasses, a student like me, worked at the front desk, and an older woman on the phone sat at another smaller desk behind the main one. Offices lined the walls to the left, and despite it being the first day of

school, we were the only ones in the office. My grandmother headed to the girl and spoke to her in Spanish.

The girl regarded me as my grandmother spoke,
looked me up and down as if she were assessing me as a
threat. I was used to such looks at new schools. After a
moment, she turned around to a file cabinet against the
wall, came back and handed my grandmother a few
pieces of paper. My grandmother shuffled the papers
around, looked them over once and then handed them
to me. She pointed to the top one, a white sheet that had
a class schedule, and then showed me the school map
beneath it. She gave my arm a hard pat, which sort of
hurt, and then left without any other instructions.

Terror spread throughout my chest for a moment. At
every other school I had gone to, it had been routine: go
in alone, new schedule, go to classes, go home. No one
knew me or my mother. But Laredo was different. People
knew my grandmother and that brought attention on me.

I looked at my schedule. Well, at least I was in an art
class. My only saving grace. Besides all the advanced
classes my grandmother had enrolled me in, something
else caught my eye. My name was printed on the top,
but instead of saying "Martha George," it read, "Martha
Gonzalez." I walked up to the desk and pointed it out to
the girl.

"My last name is George, not Gonzalez."

The girl frowned. "Isn't your grandmother *Doña
María* Gonzalez?"

"Yeah. But that's not *my* last name."

She rolled her eyes as she turned around to look
through the files again. George didn't sound like a Mexican name. My mother's last name was George, too, so I
had always assumed it was my father's name and my

father wasn't Mexican. Wherever the hell George came from, it didn't matter. My name was *not* Gonzalez. My grandmother couldn't dictate my life by changing my last name to whatever she felt like.

"There's no George here. Your *abuela* said your last name was Gonzalez."

I wanted to take her stupid glasses off and stomp on them. It didn't matter what my grandmother had said, couldn't she understand that? It wasn't my name.

But it was useless to argue with the girl because she'd probably just roll those damn eyes and nothing would be accomplished. It was 7:30 so I had fifteen minutes to get to class. I asked her for directions to the library and left. After school, I'd have to have a talk with my grandmother about this name situation.

Halfway to the library, I got lost. There were so many people in the hallways that it was hard to maneuver. The noise was unbearable, and the mixture of body sprays and cologne made me want to gag.

The library was empty except for a young librarian who looked no older than me. She was small in her grey suit and overdone make-up. I think she was trying to separate herself from the students with her style choice. It could have worked if she wasn't barely five feet tall. I walked to her desk and asked if she had any books on learning Spanish. The woman gave a small laugh, but then stopped when she realized I wasn't joking. I tried not to narrow my eyes at her in annoyance, but maybe I did, because she hurriedly showed me to the right shelf and pointed out a few books.

Although the books were ten years old, they appeared brand new, which confirmed that I was probably the first person ever to attend this school and not know Spanish. Perfect. I checked out three that looked easy to understand and headed to my first class. I had four minutes to get there.

When I made it to the correct wing of the building, the halls were clearing up. I was searching for room 3B, when someone grabbed me from behind and shoved me into a girl's bathroom.

"Hey!" I said.

When I got my balance, I saw pink tile and three stalls with white paint peeling off the doors. I was surrounded by three tough-looking girls, led by the girl I saw leaving grandmother's house a few days ago. She stood a few feet in front of the group with the most pissed off I'm-so-ready-to-kick-your-ass look, complete with penciled-in eyebrows, an overabundance of mascara and eyeliner and lips that had been outlined in dark red lip liner but had not been filled in with lipstick.

Her hair was parted down the middle and slicked down with gel. Without her weird make-up, she could probably be pretty with her small, button nose and almond-shaped eyes. She reminded me of my mother, but at least my mother didn't look like a scary Chucky doll. The other girls stood around the dark-eyed girl and sported the same style in make-up and clothes.

I'd been in a lot of fights when I was younger—everyone wanted to mess with the new girl. But no one had ever tried to fight me the first day of school. Something about the way this girl looked at me, how she had looked at me at church—this was personal, at least for her.

"What's your problem?" I asked.

The black-eyed girl spoke in Spanish and took a step toward me. I might have been more scared if I knew what the hell she was saying. It was like listening to the

Tasmanian devil, slobbering and yapping about God knew what.

"I don't know what you're saying," I said.

The girl stopped and tilted her head for a moment. And then she laughed, triggering laughter from her minions, like this was a bad cartoon stand-off.

"Look, *chicas*, we got a *güera* here with us." They laughed again. "That *bruja* grandmother of yours chose a *güera* over me?"

"What are you talking about?"

The girl took a step closer to me, followed by the three other girls. Instinctively, I took a step back. I could take on one, but four . . . I'd be dead.

"What? You don't understand English either, *fea?*"

"Look, I don't know what you're talking, but I need to get to class."

I tried to sidestep around her and her friends, but she stopped me by shoving me up against the wall. As my back hit the cold tile, I smelled the strong fruit-scented perfume she must have bathed in that morning. My heart beat a little faster. Could I not get a freaking break this week?

"You can leave when I say you can leave, *puta*, you hear me?"

I didn't respond. I focused on keeping my face under control. Flat with no emotion.

"Listen, you tell that *bruja* of yours she better watch her back. And you, *fea,* stay out of my way. I run this school, and I'm more than happy to beat your ass. But since it's the first day, you get a free pass."

She slapped the wall right by my head to emphasize her threat. I flinched, which made her smile. She gave me one more intense look, bared her teeth and then walked out of the bathroom followed by her friends.

A nervous sweat broke out on my neck. I leaned back on the wall for support. So now my grandmother's enemies were my enemies? This family thing was not what I had expected. I leaned my head against the cool tile.

A shrill bell echoed in the bathroom.

"Damn it." I banged my fists backwards against the wall, then headed to my first class.

I finally found room 3B. The teacher, a woman, was speaking in the front, explaining the course—Pre-Calculus. She stopped speaking and turned to look at me, as did the entire class.

Ducking my head, I said, "Sorry," and hurried to a seat in the back.

If only that could have been enough.

"You're late," the teacher, Mrs. Herrera, said.

Had I not just said sorry? I sat down at a desk.

Mrs. Herrera, with her bird-like features, stared at me pointedly, her cheeks drawn in and her eyes squinting behind her glasses. She was waiting for me to respond, but I didn't. The less one said, the better. That had always been the case for me at other schools.

A guy next to me snickered behind his hand. I wanted to turn and give him a nasty look but I held back the urge. Finally, Mrs. Herrera realized I wasn't going to answer. She grabbed a clipboard.

"Name?"

"Martha George."

She looked through the list. "I don't have a George."

"Gonzalez then." Stupid grandmother.

"Gonzalez with a 'z,' not as common. Is your older sister Brenda?" Mrs. Herrera's lips turned down slightly. Guess she didn't like Brenda either.

"No. I just moved here so . . . "

Her head turned to the side in thought. "Wait, are you *la nieta de* María Gonzalez that just moved here?" Mrs. Herrera's voice changed. It didn't sound so disapproving anymore.

My classmates turned in their seats and stared at me. Not again. "What?"

I wanted to hide behind my hair. More Spanish. Confused lines appeared on Mrs. Herrera's forehead. She was slowly figuring it out.

"You are Doña María's granddaughter, yes?"

I nodded yes.

Mrs. Herrera smiled, and her cold features softened. She hurriedly walked to me and held out her hand. "Welcome, Martha. I'm so glad to have you in my class."

I shook her hand, my cheeks burning with all the attention. When I pulled my hand back, I murmured, "Thank you."

She added, "And don't worry about your tardiness. It's your first day here." With a last smile, she returned to the front and began speaking again about the course but with a newfound bit of excitement in her voice and gestures.

I wanted to hide, to run out of the classroom. For the rest of the period, my classmates stared at me or whispered with neighbors, giving me furtive glances over their shoulders. I even heard one girl sitting two seats in front of me say, "I can't believe she can't speak . . . " only to be interrupted by her neighbor who said, "I know! *Loca.*"

At times, Mrs. Herrera would translate something she had said in English to Spanish. Other times, students would raise their hand and ask a question in Spanish and she would respond in Spanish. Then she would turn to me and translate everything that had been said in Spanish to English.

"Martha, José asked how many tests I would give this semester. The answer is four."

Death would have been so much sweeter than the embarrassment I suffered.

In each class that morning, it felt like everyone whispered as soon as I entered. I suspected they spoke about the incident with the black-eyed girl or my relation to my grandmother. A few of the teachers made comments when they called my name out. "Oh! You're *Doña María*'s granddaughter?" Being quiet and keeping my head down was not going to allow me to be invisible at this school.

This was the second worst day of my life. The first: being left in Laredo.

At lunch, the cafeteria was filled with students, even though some went onto the lawn to eat their lunch. Kids sat grouped around their plastic trays. Most walked from table to table and yelled at each other from across the room. A few monitors walked around trying to keep the peace.

I didn't even get a chance to look around the cafeteria for an empty seat after I grabbed a tray of food because a short girl with a jet black ponytail that showed off her deep widow's peak walked up to me.

"Martha?"

"Yeah?"

"I'm your *prima* . . . Laura. *Vámonos*. You can sit with me."

Before I responded she headed in the direction of a table on the far wall.

When I caught up to her, I asked, "What's *'vamanus?'*"

"I thought it was just a rumor that you couldn't speak Spanish."

"Not this time." There was an edge to my voice.

Why did everyone assume that I should know Spanish? Was I the only Mexican in the world who didn't know how to speak Spanish? What if you were orphaned and then adopted by a non-Mexican or non-Spanish-speaking family?

"*'Vámonos'* means let's go."

We came to a table and sat down. A few students sat at the end, so we had the space to ourselves.

"So, you're my cousin?"

"Yeah, my *abuelo* was your *abuela*'s brother, but he died five years ago."

"So *'abuelo'* is grandfather?"

"Yep. And *'abuela'* is grandmother."

We started eating our lunch. "So how come you weren't at Juanita's house yesterday?"

Laura laughed. "Our whole *familia* couldn't even fit in this cafeteria. Besides my mom and I sort of aren't welcome." She stuck her fork in a peach and took a bite.

"What do you mean 'sort of'?"

"Okay . . . we're not welcome at all."

"Why?"

She ate another peach then shrugged. "Your grandmother doesn't like my mom."

"What did your mom do?"

"She didn't do anything," Laura said quickly, then a little unsurely, "at least, I don't think so. I really don't know why your *abuela* doesn't like my mom. Just that they've always had something going on for as long as I can remember."

"And you and I hanging out at lunch aren't going to cause the next Civil War?"

She smiled. "Would you care if it did?"

As I was about to answer, a loud crash echoed through the cafeteria, followed by laughter. I turned around to find the black-eyed girl surrounded by her friends and a bunch of tough-looking guys wearing grey, button-up shirts and slicked-back hair. They sat on top of a few tables and were laughing at a girl who had dropped her tray. One boy who chewed on a cigarette stood up and did an impression of the girl dropping her tray. Everyone laughed, and he sat back down and kissed the black-eyed girl.

The girl who had dropped her tray looked as if she was trying not to cry as she picked her food off the floor. Her friends had already left her and her embarrassment behind.

I turned around disgusted and shook my head. Laura was looking closely at me.

"I also heard Marcela is pissed at you," she said.

"You hear a lot of things. So, the witch's name is Marcela?"

She nodded.

"What's her problem?" I asked.

"You mean, why is she such a bitch?"

"Yes!"

Laura laughed. "She used to be . . . " Laura blew air into her cheeks.

"Fat?"

She laughed again. "Yeah. Sort of teased when we were younger. Then around junior high she started hanging out with these real tough *cholas* that were in high school and suddenly she starts losing the weight and fighting everyone who ever made fun of her, and it just escalated from there."

"So the bullied becomes the bully. How nice."

"You're funny," she said, adding, "but you know, it's not good to be on her bad side. But you couldn't help that, could you?"

"I couldn't help it? I don't even know her. Why does she have a problem with me?"

Laura leaned closer and lowered her voice. "You know how your *abuela* is a *curandera?*"

My thoughts went back to what Gloria had said. I nodded yes.

"Well, Gloria has been telling people that Marcela went to your *abuela* and asked to be her apprentice, but Doña María turned her down."

"Apprentice? You mean Marcela wants to be a *curand* . . . what my grandmother is? Why?"

Laura bit into her sandwich and then answered after a few chews. "If you have the gift, you have the gift, and your *abuela* is the best *curandera* around. Anyway, I wouldn't put my life in Marcela's hands. Ever. Your *abuela* has never taken an apprentice before. Until you."

I put down the apple I was about to bite into. "Me? No, no, I'm not her apprentice I'm just living with her. Wasn't even my choice."

"That's not what Marcela thinks, and that's all that matters."

She looked over my shoulder. I turned around to see Marcela's eyes had found me all the way from across the cafeteria. It was as if she knew that at that exact moment we were speaking about her. All hope of her forgetting about me was ridiculous. I had an enemy, and she wasn't going away.

School ended with my backpack full to the brim with beaten-down textbooks, homework and the Spanish books. When the last bell rang, I headed to the front yard of the school, nervous because I only remembered then that my grandmother hadn't said whether she would be there to walk home with me. When I stepped out the front doors, I spotted her standing by the flagpole with a straw hat and her braid draped over her shoulder. When she saw me she turned around and started walking to the house. I had to run with the twenty pounds strapped to my back.

If I ever caught up to the old lady, I might have confronted her about my new name or about Marcela.

The remainder of the week went something like this: I woke up, went to school, returned home to do homework and studied the Spanish books I had checked out. My first task was to memorize a few words before I started using them. I tried to pick up the pattern and movement of the language by listening to my grandmother and Gloria speak at dinner, which was like trying to identify which musical note went with what sound.

"*Ay, Dios mío, ¿te enteraste de lo que pasó con Lupe?*" Gloria said.

Gloria was talking about someone named Lupe and did so as a question.

"*No, ¿qué pasó?*" My grandmother took a bite of bread. 'No' was the same in both languages. Another question.

"*Su esposo la está dejando por una mujer más joven,*" Gloria said.

Abuela gasped, then said, "*¡Ay, no!*"

"*En serio. Me lo comentó Doña Teresa en la iglesia.*"

Church! I remembered *iglesia* meant church. Something about church . . .

"*¡No puede ser!*" Abuela replied.

"*Dios nos libre. Esas mujeres no son buenas.*"

I was lost. They spoke so fast: up and down, syllable after syllable, rolling the r's, loud gasps and signs of the cross.

Gloria turned to me suddenly, "Don't be like these *cochinas* around here!"

My grandmother nodded in agreement while I sat chewing my *fideo*.

Oh, yeah, I was still a beginner in this language game.

Laura sat with me every day at lunch. I was a junior and she was a senior, almost exactly two years older than me to the day. She introduced me to some of her friends, and halfway through the week they came and sat with us during lunch. The twins, Bella and Estrella, drove me insane, and many days I wished they had never joined us at all. No other students were keen on getting to know me. I didn't know if it was because I was new, because of my grandmother or because of Marcela.

Every time I saw Marcela with her boyfriend, Eduardo, or her group of thugs, I went in the opposite direction. It wasn't that I was scared. It was because Laura was right: Marcela would probably use every chance she had to get back at me, no matter how ridiculous her thoughts on my non-existent apprenticeship were. And it was a ridiculous thought. Voodoo, mumbo jumbo healing magic? Like my grandmother could *really* heal someone with smelly potions. *Cura*—that "c" word . . . I'd never heard of such a thing. And why would I want to be apprentice to my grandmother, anyway? I lived with the lady, and spending more time with her did not appeal to me.

I decided against asking my grandmother about why she hadn't taken Marcela as an apprentice. First of all, I couldn't ask her in Spanish. Within that first week, I had only advanced to small greetings, numbers, colors and items around the house, so that was out of the question. And I kept having trouble with words and their gender. That was the weirdest thing about Spanish: words were either male or female. I thought I had it figured out, though. For instance, anything ending in "o" was masculine and anything ending in "a" was feminine, but then Spanish would switch it up on me. Like you would think "*día*," or day, was female but it was actually male, and you had to say *buenos días* and not *buenas días*. And it was the opposite for "night." The "o" and "a" were kicking my ass.

Second, it wasn't hard to guess why my grandmother hadn't chosen Marcela: she was a bully, and wasn't the kind of person that would do well with instruction. She had her own agenda. And Marcela's problem with me, well, what went on between Marcela and me was between Marcela and me. I'd handle it. She looked scary, but, really, what could she do? Laura had mentioned some rumor about Marcela stabbing someone, but that sounded a little too far-fetched to me. She would have been sent to jail . . . right?

On the Friday of my first week of school, during study period, I got a bathroom pass and was on my way there, when something caught my eye. In the hallway, there were two large, glass display cases that I hadn't really taken note of before. Because I didn't want to get back to study period to write something about the first few chapters of *The Great Gatsby*, I looked in the cases to waste some time. Besides, I'd already read the book at the last school I had attended, and I didn't relish revisiting the Gatsby and Daisy drama. I had enough drama of my own.

One display case was filled with academic awards—certificates, trophies for the debate team, pictures of the Math Club at a competition, a plaque presented by the governor for "Most Improved School in South Texas." Most of the items were ten years old or older. It seemed the school had not been successful in anything lately.

The second case was sports related, with a faded letterman jacket, trophies, a picture of a winning baseball team and pictures of the homecoming queens and kings and their courts. I'd never been to a homecoming, although I had witnessed girls and boys at my previous school vying for the court by hanging posters in the hallways and handing out candy between classes for a vote. Part of me liked to think it was pathetic. It was a popularity vote. However, a small part of me secretly wished to be a part of homecoming elections, have lots of friends, be liked by many, admired as pretty . . . whatever. Didn't everyone secretly wish the same thing at some time or another?

The homecoming court pictures ranged from last year all the way back to the 1960s. Some were colored photos, some were in black and white. The frames and photos dating back to the mid-1960s were larger than the recent ones. When I got to the picture of the homecoming queen of 1971, I did a double take. My hands reached forward but were stopped by glass.

I barely recognized her in the photo. Her face was younger and smoother, and her hair, jet black, had been styled in large curls that fell to her waist. She wore a sequined dress that fit her curvy frame perfectly, so that it fell like a waterfall to her feet. And she smiled! She actually smiled without the lies around the edges of her lips, a truthful smile—something I had rarely witnessed. The crown stood tall on her head, and in her arms she held a large bouquet of roses. My mother had been homecoming queen when she was seventeen.

Unlike the other, more formal photographs of the homecoming court with the king and queen surrounded by the princes and princesses, this picture was a candid shot with my mother looking up at the football stands. It must have been the moment just after she'd been crowned. On her right stood the king who, instead of looking where my mother was, was caught by the camera looking at her. And on my mother's right side was another girl with straight hair and her arm around my mother's shoulders, giving her a congratulatory hug. She had a crown half the size of my mother's on her head. The girl's face looked worn and her skin stretched thinly over bony cheeks, making her large, bug eyes more pronounced.

At the bottom of the frame an engraved plate read:

Left to Right: Senior Princess: Carlita Juarez; Homecoming Queen: Junior, Rosa Gonzalez; Homecoming King: Senior, Jorge Valdez

I stared at the photograph and tried to imagine a mother I had never known, a girl that had walked these same halls. How did my mother go from the black and white photo to the woman I had known for sixteen years? Or the woman I had never actually known. I didn't really know her. Did I? Who was she, this homecoming queen? A Big Fake? I just didn't get it. How come I had never pushed my mother to tell me about where she'd come from?

Something in me couldn't shake the questions for the rest of the day, until finally I decided that I'd rather run into the open arms of Marcela than let these questions go unanswered.

That Friday after school, I finally felt confident enough to use Spanish with my grandmother. I figured she would laugh at me or ignore me. Either way I was determined to try. I hadn't counted on Gloria coming over for dinner, but I thought, to hell with it, I'd have to speak in front of her sometime. I brought one of the Spanish books into the kitchen with me. It was more for encouragement rather than to look at. Maybe that's why my grandmother carried a Bible with her in her purse when she left the house. Encouragement.

A sweet aroma of potatoes and meat filled the kitchen. *Papas y carne.* Gloria was speaking to my grandmother as the old woman placed a glass of milk, a plate of food and a piece of chocolate cake for dessert in front of me. I ate quickly, enjoying the spicy flavors that Abuela had used. When I finished eating the meat and potatoes, I finally summoned all the courage I had and spoke my first Spanish words to Abuela.

"*Muy bueno.*"

The words felt like Jell-O in my mouth, not fully under my control as they rolled across my tongue. Gloria, who hadn't stopped talking since she had arrived, suddenly went quiet and looked at me. Her head reared back like a dog unsure of what had come across its path. I risked a glance up at my grandmother, who regarded me with an expression I couldn't quite read. It was somewhere between interest and amusement.

Gloria laughed loud. "*¿Muy bueno? Mira,* you hear her? Oh, speaking Spanish now? A real *mexicana* we have here."

My grandmother smirked, and my cheeks grew hot. Gloria continued with what she thought were witty jokes as I ate my desert.

"Repeat after me, Martha. *La chica es inteligente.*" And, "Remember, Martha, *es muy.* Not moo-ey. Nothings worse than saying it like a *gringo.*"

After the last one, my grandmother said something to her which made Gloria stop. But she continued to smile and laugh at random moments for no reason. I stifled the urge to stab her with my fork, but instead jabbed my chocolate cake. Honestly, it wasn't *that* funny. I didn't say anything else, only ate, then hurried and placed my dishes in the sink.

I was determined to say one more thing in Spanish. Gloria thought she could make fun of me? Fine, I'd throw something else in her face. So before I walked out of the kitchen, I turned around and looked at my grandmother and aunt who were speaking rapid Spanish.

Without waiting for them to stop, I interrupted them with, "*Buenos noches, señores.*" I overtly pronounced each syllable before stomping out of the kitchen and to my room.

"*¡¿Buenos?!*" My grandmother shouted in glee.

"*¡Y señores!*" Gloria exclaimed. "I thought the only *huevos* you had were in the fridge!"

They didn't stop laughing for an hour.

My Spanish continued to improve, especially with my grandmother's help. I didn't really ask her for help, but she wouldn't stop looking over my shoulder when I studied from the Spanish books at the dining room table before meals. Then she proceeded to point her finger at different things, flip the pages while I was reading and kept saying, "No, no, no. No right." Or she'd laugh at the word a book used. Like for car, she said, "*No es 'automóvil,' es 'carro.'*" Then she'd laugh again. I didn't get any studying done during those moments. That's how she forced herself into my Spanish education, which was kind of funny, since the reason I wanted to learn Spanish was to grill her about my mother.

My grandmother came up with this idea to go around the house and point out every object and give me its name. I took it a step further and wrote the names of the objects on pieces of paper and placed them on everything in the house. Soon, little white pieces of paper were taped on everything. My grandmother didn't like it, because it took away from the religious gaudiness, but in the end she allowed me my scraps of paper. On weekends, she'd quiz me by taking all of the papers off, pointing to the object for its name and waiting for my answer. For each name I got wrong, I had to scrub the floor of a room in the house. Not my idea at all. My grandmother could come up with the most creative punishments. But after three weeks, I knew hundreds of nouns, could count to infinity (or close to it), could name the colors, knew every basic greeting and the floors were entirely too clean. I had worked up to basic sentences and was starting to learn to conjugate verbs. By the middle of September, I was able to speak basic sentences to my grandmother.

At school, I tried to stay out of Marcela's way, although she made it a point to find me. If I saw her in the hallway, she'd try to trip me or say things under her breath in the Spanish I didn't know yet, or make threats in English that I *did* know and *didn't* like. I sidestepped her trips or ignored her words and kept moving. One day I was waiting for Laura at our table, when Laura slapped her tray down next to me. I jumped. Heads turned from up to three tables away.

"What's wrong?" I asked.

She glared over my shoulder at Marcela's tables, which only made her widow's peak stretch farther down her head. "*Esa puta,*" she said, "cornered me in the bathroom earlier." Laura had taught me all the bad words in Spanish weeks ago. "*Puta*" was my favorite word for Marcela.

"Wait, what? Why?"

"She wants to know what your *abuela* is teaching you. She still thinks you're her apprentice."

I put the chicken sandwich I had been holding down onto my plate. "So . . . what happened?"

She picked up her slice of pizza and took an angry bite out of it, causing grease to drip down her chin. She didn't wipe it off. "*¡Nada!* I couldn't tell her nothing, because you're not her apprentice. She didn't like that. But whatever, that's her problem. All I know is I hope your *abuela* starts teaching you to be a *curandera. Ay, Dios,* I'd love to see her face then!"

I didn't agree with Laura. Since I wasn't at home anymore during the days, the only time I saw my grandmother do her *curandera* work was on Saturdays. And even then I stayed in whoever's kitchen we were at, doing homework or reading my Spanish books. Besides, learning the *curandera*'s secret healing magic wasn't important to me. Finding out the location of my mother was at the top of my list. I'd even go look at that homecoming picture at times to keep focused.

Every once in a while I'd ask my grandmother,
"*¿Dónde está mi madre?*" Where is my mother? And she'd
purse her lips and go off on a rant that she knew I
wouldn't understand. I had to learn more. I had to become
fluent. My mother couldn't just leave me like she did. I
wanted to know why: why she left me, why she left all
those years ago, why she changed.

But what I wanted never happened—at least, not in
Laredo. I could have jumped in the Rio Grande in hopes
of floating to the ocean, and somehow, someway, I'm
sure that river would have turned me right back around
and flopped me on the front lawn of the Pepto-Bismol
casa, where my grandmother would be waiting with a
bucket of water and soap to tell me I got it all wrong
once again.

Cinco

ONE SUNDAY AFTER CHURCH, it was Juanita's turn to host the family again at her house. Her house didn't smell like dogs, like Tío Jesús' did, and wasn't miserably hot, like my cousin Elva's house. Elva, like many people in Laredo, didn't have an air conditioner, but she also refused to open windows, because "What if someone stuck their head out of the window and the window fell and sliced their head off?!" She didn't have fans because, "God forbid, someone might have their finger chopped off!" The time we were at her house, my cousins and *tías* and *tíos* had begged her to open the windows and insisted on fans until Elva, with her *loca* nature, ran at my cousin, Mario, with an ear of corn to beat him over his head. She did something similar to one or two of the *familia* each time someone suggested not having Sunday meals at her house.

Lilia was playing with dolls in the living room after we had eaten, and I was drawing her as she did. The house still smelled of *carnitas* and rice. I was beginning to like this new diet. I inhaled the sweet and spicy aftermath of our large lunch. My clothes had already captured the perfume of the food, which would only be removed with a good washing. Lilia and I were both sucking on watermelon lollipops *con chile* as we played.

"Martha, I need *mi otra muñeca*, Mimi," Lilia said. She was in the middle of a reenactment with her dolls featuring an argument she had had with some girl in Sunday school class over a crayon.

"Lilia, there's five dolls here. You don't need Mimi," I said.

She put the two dolls down and stood in front of me. "*Pero* I do. *Ella es mi favorita.*"

She was doing it again, using her cuteness to convince me otherwise. Those large brown eyes and her cute little accented voice that switched between English and Spanish so easily made me slightly jealous. She was six years old. It wasn't fair.

"Fine, go get Mimi."

"I can't. I'm busy. Could you go get her for me, *por favor?*"

Oh, a little *diablita*. "*No podría*, Lilia. You go get her."

She took out her sucker and pushed out her bottom lip. "*Trompas*," Juanita called it. "Martha! Pretty, pretty please? I can't leave *mis muñecas aquí. Los chicos* will get them." She pushed her lip out farther.

I wasn't going to win this one. Lilia was too horribly cute, and she was the only family member that I felt comfortable talking to in Spanish. If I messed up, she didn't notice, probably because we both struggled to communicate in two different languages.

"All right, okay," I said. I put down my journal and pencil and got up. She smiled and popped her lollipop back in her mouth.

The hallway had four doors. The bathroom and Lilia's room were on the left side while Tomás' room and Juanita's and her husband's were on the right. I was about to open the door to Lilia's room, when I heard voices coming from across the hall. The door was half-cracked. Juanita stood in the room, her hands on her hips and her mouth set in a firm line. I looked down the hall. No one would find me eavesdropping; most everyone was outside watching my cousins and *tíos* play a game of soccer in dress pants and their nice, leather shoes.

"What are you waiting for? You have to tell her," Juanita said. It didn't take long to figure out who she was speaking to.

"*No, no tengo que hacer nada.*" I don't have to do anything, my grandmother replied.

"You know as well as I do that Rosa didn't just abandon her here. And you're letting all this time go by. Mamá, start now. Why are you waiting?"

"*Sí, estoy haciendo algo. Le estoy enseñando español, ¿no? Le estoy dando un lugar donde quedarse, una educación y una familia. Y no le ayudes a tu hermana. Esa cochina.*" I am doing something, I'm teaching her Spanish, no? Giving her a place to stay, education, a family. And don't help your sister. That pig.

"Really, Mamá? And don't flick your wrist at me like that. Rosa is giving you what you wanted, and you know as well as I that Martha has more of the gift than either Rosa . . . "

My grandmother cut off Juanita. "*No digas su nombre.*" Don't say whose name?

Juanita put her hands through her hair in exasperation. "Mamá, you can't just let this continue. You are getting old. You need help with everything, need to pass it on and, trust me, I wish it had been me, not Rosa, who could have done that for you, but it's not. She left, and you refuse to even acknowledge the possibility of asking . . . "

My grandmother made a noise in her throat to stop Juanita.

But Juanita stared my grandmother down and said, " . . . *her*."

Who was she talking about? My mother? My grandmother remained silent.

"It's obvious, then. Martha is your only option, Mamá. Make things right—finally. *Por favor*. I can't continue watching. This has to stop. You just have to."

"*Yo siempre trato de hacer lo que pienso que es mejor*." I always try to do what I think is best.

"*Yo sé*, Mamá. *No es suficiente*."

That was enough. I opened the door. "I'm the only option for what?"

I expected my grandmother to yell, but I didn't expect it from Juanita.

"Get out, Martha! This doesn't concern you!"

"But it does . . . "

"I said out! Now!" She pointed at the door and stomped her foot at the same time.

I slammed the door and headed to the living room. Lilia wasn't happy that I didn't bring her doll, but I was too angry and intrigued at what I had heard to really care. It was clear that my grandmother and my family knew more things about my mother than they let on. How come no one told me anything? What was with all the secrets? I was sixteen years old, not a child.

Apparently, a direct approach wasn't going to get me anywhere. My grandmother refused any inquiries I made, and Juanita wouldn't go against her mother's wishes, even for her niece. But why would she? She didn't know me. I was just some stranger who had appeared abruptly in her life.

I knew a few things now. My mother hadn't abandoned me for no reason. Part of me couldn't believe it, but I wanted to at least. Juanita had a higher opinion of my mother than I or my grandmother seemed to have, so who knew what was true? Regardless, it sounded like I had some kind of gift. *Curanderismo?* Which was ridiculous. If I had *the* gift, wouldn't my grandmother have said something by now? And I had never seen my mother do anything magical. Rather, she had always made fun of the psychics on television. Even threw food at the TV a few times. Besides, I couldn't do magic or whatever my grandmother did. And that was a damn fact.

By Monday, I had two goals in mind: find the old yearbooks in the school library and then glean any information I could from them about my mother. I got the idea when picture day came around and everyone wouldn't shut up about the outfits and hairstyles they were going to sport that day.

During study hall when I asked to go to the library, my teacher, glad that anyone wanted to go, was quick to give me a pass. The halls were mostly empty, except for one white-haired janitor who was mopping when I passed. The school smelled of Pine-Sol and a hint of lemon, which reminded me of the Saturday-morning house cleanings that my grandmother made me participate in.

As I was about to push the double doors forward to go into the library, a whistle echoed through the silent corridor. It was one of those whistles that went high then low then high again, the universal whistle that says, "Hey, good looking." I turned around, hoping that the whistle wasn't for me.

Behind me stood a boy with two other guys. He wore black Dickies and a plain red T-shirt. The boys stared at me, smiling, and looked me up and down, taking in my legs in the cut off shorts I wore. I immediately regretted my outfit choice.

"*¿Cómo te llamas, hermosa?*" The boy in the red T-shirt said, then licked his lips.

I wanted to say something, but nothing came out of my mouth. My tank top felt too tight, and the back of my neck felt hot and sweaty. I looked behind the boy and his friends for the janitor, but he must have walked off because I was alone.

"Look! The girl lost her voice," the tall guy behind the boy in the red T-shirt said.

Okay, maybe I had. But whereas my mother basked in male attention, I ran from it. At least I ran from boys and their attention *that* year of high school.

I didn't like it when men called out to me or whistled at me like I was a damn dog. Especially not from *this* particular guy.

"Come here, I want to talk to you," the boy with the red T-shirt said, then puckered his lips and made a kissing noise

Finally, I found my nerves. "Oh, shut up!"

I felt my legs again and, without hesitation, went through the double doors into the library, my stomach a mess of knots. Catcalls rang out after me. I took a moment, caught my breath. *Great, great, great.* I peeked out the window and saw the boys walking down the hall away from me. This wasn't good. The guy who had whistled at me was Eduardo, Marcela's boyfriend.

I found the yearbooks fairly easily. After finding a corner among the bookshelves, I spread the four yearbooks out around me so I could easily flip through the crisp, glossy pages. It was the first time I had ever looked through a yearbook. We couldn't afford to buy one for me the last two years and even if we had, why would I buy memories of a year of people that I didn't know and who didn't know me? And for that matter, I hated taking pictures: my hair was never fixed or I had a stupid smile on my face each time the camera flashed. It just looked forced. If there happened to be a picture of me in a yearbook, I did not want to know.

Based on the first three yearbooks, my mother was pretty popular. In every single picture, whether it was a still class photo or a candid shot, my mother looked happy. She had been involved not only in student council and theater but also softball. I loved the candid pictures the most, although seeing her wide, genuine smile hurt since she had shared only a few with me. In almost every picture with my mother was the girl, the princess from the homecoming court photograph, Carlita Juárez.

Carlita was a year older than my mother. They were in the same clubs together, though, and always stood next to each other in every photograph. By the time my mother was a junior, Jorge Valdez, the homecoming king, began to pop up in a few pictures too, always with his hands around my mother's waist or holding *her* hand. He must have been her boyfriend. My mother had friends and a boyfriend. I never even had the chance to have friends.

We moved so much, and I learned that most people didn't like forming bonds with the new girl. Boyfriends were a big no for me, too. Crushes and flings were okay, but boyfriends involved having to make up excuses as to why I never wanted one to meet my mother or come to whatever dirty trash apartment we lived in. Besides, I had my drawings. It may sound pathetic, but I never noticed how alone I was when I had a pencil and a paper to keep me company.

In my mother's senior year, there were only three photos of her in the entire book—I know because I checked five times, scanning every face and every name. By the time I was done, my fingers ached with paper cuts thanks to the crisp, thick pages. One of the pictures was her class photo. In the other two pictures my mother stood alone in photographs. Maybe because Carlita and Jorge had graduated her junior year? My mother smiled, but now instead of the genuine smile, it had a small hint of the smile she had used for so many years with me. Was this when the Big Fake started? Had something gone wrong? So her friends weren't at school with her any longer, but that didn't mean my mother should want to flee Laredo. Something was still missing.

I'd been in the library for forty minutes and had to get back to study hall. On my way back, I wondered where Carlita and Jorge were now.

Did they live in Laredo still?

The next day brought a few clouds—a miracle in Laredo. Laura and I decided to eat outside on the pavilion. We sat at one of the picnic tables enjoying the mildly hot afternoon. There was even a slight breeze—a magical unicorn in the heat-driven weather of Laredo. Today had to be the closest thing to paradise in this city.

It would have been perfect if Laura could have stopped her incessant chatter about some guy named

Rafi. It'd been going on for twenty minutes already. "So Maya told me *que* Rafi likes me, *pero no sé. Espero* that it's true, you know? He's a junior and . . . " Her words fell off and her eyes grew big at something behind me while her mouth opened slightly.

I turned to find Marcela walking towards us, followed by her group of friends.

"*¡Ay, puta! Te he estado buscando, güera fea.*" I've been looking for you, ugly white girl.

At that point, I understood a lot more Spanish than I could speak. I usually filled in the words that I didn't know by guessing.

Marcela yelled loud enough so that everyone outside turned and stared. I felt the chant "fight, fight!" hanging in the air, ready to be taken up by on-lookers. I stood up, glad that I was a few inches taller. Marcela and her bullshit had gotten on my last nerve. It didn't look like I could avoid her any longer.

"*¿Qué quieres?*" I asked her.

She hesitated, surprised that I spoke Spanish. "Oh, you speak Spanish now? Decided you want to be like us *mexicanos*? Learn to speak Spanish and then steal our boyfriends? And you ask what *I* want?"

"I don't want your boyfriend. At all."

I tried to turn around and sit but she grabbed my arm and turned me back to her. As soon as her hand touched me, my skin burned beneath her palm. Taken by surprise, I let out a slight hiss of pain. What the hell was that? I pulled my arm out of her grasp. Before I looked at my arm, she spoke.

"I'm not done talking with you." Marcela's eyes looked even more intimidating when she was angry because her thick, black eyeliner framed the black fire that danced within them. "Keep your dirty hands away from *mi novio*. You better be glad we're at school or I'd kick your ass so . . . "

"Like I said: I don't want your boyfriend, Marcela. He was the one hitting on me, and if you have a problem with it, you can turn around and tell him."

Marcela's face was red with anger, which shone through the layer of white powder she had caked on. I looked over her shoulder. She turned around.

Eduardo and his friends watched. His friends slapped him on the back and laughed.

Marcela turned back to me and muttered, "To hell with it."

She was about to jump on me, when a teacher's voice rang out. "Hey! What are you doing? Break it up, break it up!"

A crowd had formed around us, and a young male teacher pushed through to us. Marcela gave me one last look before turning around and stomping toward her boyfriend. I sat down, hoping the teacher would just let it go. Lucky for me, he was more concerned with dispersing the crowd.

"*¡Perra desgraciada!*" I said and pushed my tray forward so hard that it would have fallen off the table if Laura hadn't caught it.

"Whoa. Chill out. *Perra desgraciada* is right, but who taught you that?"

I shook my head, not wanting to answer. I had heard my grandmother say it when Gloria brought up Laura's mother's name one evening at dinner.

"Hey, what's that?" She pointed to my arm.

I looked down and felt a throbbing pain. It looked as if my arm had been burned, but in the exact outline of

Marcela's fingers. The skin was red and a few blisters were forming.

Laura made the sign of a cross. "Does it hurt?"

"Kind of. Why'd you do the cross thing?"

"Marcela did that, huh? That's not," she faltered for the right word, "good. That's *bruja* work."

"*¿Bruja?*" Marcela had called Abuela that before, but I wasn't sure what it meant.

"Witch," Laura whispered.

I was going to say something like "bitch." Especially since I didn't believe in witches.

By my last class, the burn had spread out so it didn't look like human fingers so much but more like a Sasquatch claw, and the skin had risen into a thin layer of blister. Every time I moved my arm, it was followed by an involuntary hiss, or a cuss word, especially when I accidentally rubbed up against something.

My physics teacher asked me if I needed to go to the nurse when she noticed the red welts. I shook my head "no" and said it was hives from an allergy. I don't think she bought it.

I thought about hiding it before I went home, but my grandmother was a dog that sniffed out trouble. So what would be the point?

When I returned home, Abuela was grating cheese with her back to the door. She suddenly turned as soon as I had taken a couple of steps.

"*¿Qué es eso?*"

Too worn out to speak in Spanish, I replied in English. "What's what?" I was not in the mood to have this discussion with my grandmother. Especially not about Marcela.

"*¡Eso! ¿Quién te hizo eso.*" That! Who did that to you?

She rushed over to me and took hold of my arm tenderly. I pulled my arm away, trying not to wince or groan in pain. Something like this wouldn't have happened if I had still been with my mother.

"*¿Dónde está mi madre?*"

My grandmother looked up, "*¿Qué? ¿Por qué me preguntas eso? Mira tu brazo. ¿Quién lo hizo?*" What? Why are you asking about that? Look at your arm. Who did that?

"*No entiendo.*" I pretended like I didn't understand her Spanish.

I kept my lips shut and refused to answer, which only infuriated her. If my grandmother wouldn't tell me her secrets, then I wouldn't tell her mine. Two could play the secret game.

My grandmother dropped my arm, turned on her heel and went to the counter. She pulled out a bottle of some kind of oil and returned to where I now sat at the kitchen table. Without saying anything, she squirted oil on the burn. I hissed and pulled my arm back with the sting of the liquid.

"Gah dang it!"

My grandmother didn't say anything as she returned the oil to the cabinet. I got up, headed straight to my room and didn't come out the rest of the night. My grandmother didn't even ask if I wanted dinner.

The next morning the burn was gone. The annoyed and frustrated look my grandmother had had the night before was replaced with something else, a look I hadn't seen before. It was resignation.

That Saturday morning we didn't go on my grandmother's rounds. Right after breakfast, she walked from the house, straight to the Cadillac and got in without saying a word. I climbed in the passenger side.

"*¿Adónde vamos?*" Where are we going? I asked after closing the car door.

She started the car. "*¿Por qué siempre haces preguntas*"? Why do you always ask questions?

By now, my Spanish was developed enough that I was able to have conversations with my grandmother and actually understand her. Which was great . . . sometimes.

I opened my mouth to respond, but she held up her right index finger before putting the car in drive and heading out.

Why do I ask questions? Why don't you ever answer anything?

I buckled my seatbelt. Whatever. I was just glad that we weren't walking around in the heat. It was early October and the temperature was still in the 100s. Driving was faster than walking, and even if we were going to some unknown destination, it was worth the mystery.

My grandmother didn't turn on the radio. Our music was the sounds of the neighborhood coming through the rolled-down windows: children playing, the rush of the wind created by the car and the rumble of the wheels on the road.

We didn't drive far, only a few blocks into a different neighborhood, to a house painted a burnt orange. My grandmother hopped out, and I followed her. We were met on the front porch by a frantic man with a large, bushy mustache that curled slightly at the ends. His face was slick with worry and sweat. He was young, perhaps thirty. His hair went every which way as if he had been tugging at it.

"Doña María?" he said to my grandmother.

"*Sí*, where is Señora Flores?" she replied in Spanish.

"In the bedroom. Hurry, please. My wife is . . . "

The man wasn't even able to finish his sentence when a cry echoed through the house. It was the cry of a woman in agonizing pain, loud and long. I froze, and the man groaned and became more agitated, pulling at his hair as he doubled over, then shot back up.

"Ay, *Dios, por favor, señora*. It's all my fault."

My grandmother hushed the man, grabbed my arm and pulled me into the house and down the hall to a closed door. We left the man on the porch, groaning. Usually I would sit in the kitchen with the patient's family or alone, so I didn't understand why my grandmother was taking me with her.

"No, I don't want to," I said trying to turn around.

My grandmother's grip on my shirt tightened, whipping me back. There was a lady yelling like a banshee behind that door. I didn't want to go in there.

"*Vamos*," my grandmother said as she opened the door.

I was instantly overcome with the metallic stench of blood, sour sweat and other fluids.

A woman sat up in a bed on her elbows and looked at us. Her hair was plastered to her face with sweat, and she wore a blue sleeping gown pushed up over her extended belly past her waist. Her knees were raised, and in between her legs sat an older woman with streaks of gray in her hair. The old woman's head and body blocked an area of the sweating pregnant woman that I wasn't even aware of on myself. The woman on the bed groaned, threw her head back, ground her teeth and groaned again. The pregnant woman's knuckles were white as salt, gripping the sheets.

"Who are you? Out, out now!" the pregnant woman yelled in English,

I flinched and covered my nose with my hand. I tried turning again to leave, but my grandmother, ignoring the pregnant woman's shout, kept a tight grip on my shirt and pulled me forward.

"*Bueno,* Señora Flores. How is everything going?" my grandmother asked in Spanish to the old woman sitting between the pregnant woman's legs.

Señora Flores turned to us and just then, I got a glimpse of something blood-red between the pregnant woman's legs. I turned my head away, embarrassed.

Also in Spanish, Señora Flores replied, "It's a big one. Is the girl ready?"

"*Sí.*" My grandmother replied, then turned to me, letting go of my shoulder. "Martha, *ayuda.*"

"Help with what?" I said.

The woman giving birth screamed through her teeth.

My grandmother pursed her lips and dragged me over to a wash bowl sitting in the corner. She made me wash my hands with soap and water, then pushed me to Señora Flores. *What the hell was going on?*

I tried not to look at the woman's spread legs when I stood next to her, but it was hard not to. I didn't want to see this . . . *ever.*

Señora Flores stood up and gestured for me to take her place on the wooden stool she'd just been sitting on. I sat down and gripped the seat of the stool with both hands. I looked up at Señora Flores. She was larger in her mid-section than my grandmother, but her eyes were kind and she was calm in the chaos that surrounded her.

Señora Flores asked in Spanish, "Are you ready?"

"Ready for what?" I said, fumbling over the language I had been practicing for months.

She grabbed my hands and pulled me over in front of the pregnant woman's spread legs. *Ay, Dios mío.* The smell was worse this close. Bile rose in my throat. I didn't want to look. Didn't want to get any closer. But Señora Flores grabbed my wrists and pulled me so that I was directly in front of the pregnant woman. Then she pulled a chair over and sat down next to me.

"Are you serious? No, I . . . I . . . No, I . . . "

Oh, God. What was I about to do? Deliver a kid?

"Tell her to push." This lady was as crazy as my grandmother.

I shook my head. "I can't, I don't know what I'm doing."

"Martha, just do as she says. *¡Híjole!*" my grandmother said.

Señora Flores ignored my grandmother and said, "I'm here. All you have to say is 'push.'"

Something about her eyes, her composure through the screams, calmed me. I nodded a few times, took a deep breath. And then something happened. A thrill ran through me, opening up something closed off inside me.

I said, "*Empuja.* Push," but it wasn't loud enough, so Señora Flores urged me to say it again. I did and the pregnant woman listened.

The top of the baby's head appeared and I caught, turned and pulled the child from her mother without Señora Flores' help. The baby wasn't even in my arms for a few seconds, when she started to cry. Instantly, I placed my knuckle in the little girl's mouth, and she began sucking on it, quieting. How did I know to do that?

Señora Flores who was in the process of cutting the umbilical cord asked me, "Have you ever delivered a baby before?"

I laughed, surprising myself, then said, "No."

God, that was a rush! For a moment, with the child in my hands, I forgot about the mother who lay sighing and panting on the bed now.

"Have you ever even held a baby?" Señora Flores asked.

I thought for a moment, then replied, "No," again.

She smiled at me, then looked at my grandmother in the corner and gave her a nod.

After handing the baby girl to her mother, Señora Flores showed me how to soothe the afterbirth from the mother by kneading the mother's stomach so that it came out on its own. Although it was a gross and messy ordeal, I barely noticed and was proud that I didn't gag when she handed my grandmother a jar filled with the afterbirth. I had forgotten about my grandmother, for the most part engrossed in everything Señora Flores was doing to help the mother recover and check the child's health.

An hour later we left, I in a T-shirt my grandmother had brought in her bag. The shirt I had on before was covered in blood and other unmentionable substances. Abuela said she could wash it all out without leaving a stain.

In the car, I sank into the seat, suddenly drained, as if I had just scrubbed Abuela's entire house without a break. I was tired but not too tired to question my grandmother as we drove.

"What was that about?"

This had to be about *curanderismo*. What other reason
would she have brought me there? It wasn't like knowing
how to help bring a child into the world was something
every girl learned in order to become a woman. At least
not in this century, right? It could have been some weird,
Laredo Mexican girl's rite of passage, for all I knew.

Her sagging cheeks rose in a smile. "You did good,
granddaughter."

Surprised by her praise, I couldn't help but smile.
"Señora Flores is a *curandera*?"

My grandmother nodded. "*Una partera*, a midwife.
She helps women who are pregnant."

"That's her job?"

She nodded yes in response.

"So . . . are you a midwife, too?"

My grandmother snorted. "No. I do more than help
pregnant women."

"Like what? And you still haven't said what that was
all about?"

"You still don't appreciate praise, *nieta*."

Typical Abuela response. "Where are we going now?"

"To see a *yerbero*."

"What's a *yerbero*?"

"You'll see."

I leaned back onto the hot leather seat, letting the
warm Laredo air blow my hair off my face.

The *yerbero* was a herb specialist, an old graying man
with dark, leathery skin and maybe some African ances-
try. Señor Díaz, whose hands shook slightly except when
he was making his concoctions, spoke very low and slow,
so much so that I had to get closer with each word. For
some reason, I instantly liked him. When he smiled, his

wrinkles cracked so that thousands of latte colored lines appeared on his face and his surprisingly straight, white teeth stood out. Something about him was genuine and truthful.

Hundreds of plants filled his one-bedroom home and overflowed into his front and back lawn. As we walked through his house, he introduced me to his plants. My grandmother stayed in the kitchen.

"This is Charlotte," he said as he touched the leaves of a large plant with small, heart-shaped leaves, turning them different ways, putting his face close to see them better. "See how thick the stalks are? That means she's healthy enough to do her job."

"Job?"

"Charlotte's leaves can help with stomach aches when put in a tea. Now, you feel them."

I smiled. The stalks did feel strong, never mind that I wasn't sure what weak stalks felt like.

Señor Díaz loved his plants more than anything. He told me he had had an apprentice once, his son, but he had moved to Mexico with his wife and become a *yerbero* in a small town. Señor Díaz asked me to touch the plants and even the soil in the pots.

"Now speak to it."

"The plant?"

"How else will it know how to grow?"

I felt somewhat ridiculous, but I did what he asked. "Um . . . " I looked at him.

He nodded smiling.

"Grow strong, um, please?" I whispered to the plant.

Later, while we looked at a big, spiky plant that sat inside his bedroom, a woman came for help, to rid herself of a red rash on her hand. He examined her, then showed it to me. Small, circular dots covered the top of her hand. They clustered close together and were flat on her skin. The woman had been scratching them because a few were bright red and a little bloodied.

"What do you think, *m'ija?*"

I was taken back when he called me *m'ija,* "my daughter," and even more so because he had asked me what I thought. That never happened with adults.

"I really don't know. I've never seen anything like it. What is it?"

He shrugged. "Nothing but a rash, though you will find that rashes look different on each person. What matters most is how we heal it. Choose the leaves and we will make something for her."

"You want me to choose the leaves? There are thousands of plants. You know how to cure it, not me."

"I trust you. Now hurry, more people will come soon, and I don't want to get behind," he said.

I turned slowly on my heel, catching my grandmother's eye. I mouthed, "What do I do?"

"Do as he says," she said.

Thanks for the help. I maneuvered between the plants, letting my hands fall to my side and brush over the leaves just as Señor Díaz had. Maybe, it'd help?

I chose two leaves from a purple plant that sat on the TV in the living room, one small pea pod from a plant on top of the refrigerator, and as I was about to hand them to Señor Díaz, I saw a large red plant on the back porch. I don't know why, but I ran outside, plucked a leaf and ran back in to give Señor Díaz my picks.

He put them in his palm and felt them. He hummed in his throat as he rubbed the leaves. The patient sat in the living room, nursing her hand, so she didn't watch me squirm.

"Ah!" He winked at my grandmother in the corner.

She sighed. Not a sad sigh or a mad sigh, just a . . . sigh. I couldn't really read her expression.

"I got it wrong, huh?"

"Actually, you surprised me with what you chose. This will work."

Señor Díaz showed me how to cut, squeeze and grind the leaves with holy water, soil and egg to make a thick, sandy paste to place on the woman's hand.

When we left, Señor Díaz told me I was welcome back anytime and that he would be glad to teach me the secrets of his plants. I thanked him and surprised myself when I gave him a hug. He laughed and patted my back. Part of me wished he was my grandfather. Even though I was given a family, I'd never had a father or a grandfather. I never would. Gloria had told me a month earlier that my grandfather had died in the Korean War. Or at least that's what everyone believed, since he never returned home.

As soon as we got in the car, Abuela turned to me and told me to be quiet and not to ask questions, because she had some thinking to do. I didn't argue. My mind and body exhausted, I fell asleep on the way home. That night, eating *carne con chile rojo* and rice with Gloria, I decided my grandmother had had enough time to think.

"So Señora Flores and Señor Díaz . . . does this mean . . . ?"

"You went to see them? Why?" Gloria asked my grandmother.

"You know why," my grandmother said to Gloria. Before Gloria responded, Abuela put her fork down, leaned back and looked at me. "Yes," she paused, sighing, "You are going to learn *curanderismo*."

I placed my cup of milk down on the table, not caring that my mouth burned from the spicy red chile. Hearing my thoughts confirmed was more disconcerting than I thought it would be. I didn't know what to think. Gloria dropped her fork, and it clanged loudly against her plate.

Before I could speak, Gloria did. "Are you crazy, sister? Look what happened last time."

My grandmother narrowed her eyes at Gloria, the same angry look that she had given to Juanita the other day when they were speaking about my mother.

"What happened last time?" I said.

"Why would you bring that up?" Abuela said through clenched teeth to Gloria.

Gloria flipped her hand sideways twice at Abuela, as if saying, "Forget it. The girl just learned Spanish. She doesn't know a thing yet."

This was getting annoying. Couldn't someone answer me? I spoke a little louder, directing my attention to Abuela. "Why now? Why teach me now?"

Abuela opened her mouth, then closed it.

Gloria spoke first, "Yes, María, you knew she had the gift the whole time . . . Why now?"

"*¡Ay, chingao!*" Abuela looked like she wanted to stab Gloria with her fork.

"What? Why didn't you tell me?" I asked Abuela.

Abuela gave Gloria one last glare, then stuck her fork in a piece of steak. "Just because you have a gift doesn't mean you should learn *curanderismo*. You think everyone who has a gift uses it?" She took a bite, not looking at me.

"So what? Today was a test? If you knew, why did I need to do that stuff?"

"To see what areas you might have a natural affinity in."

Something hit me. "Did my mother know? About me? And this . . . gift?"

Gloria let out a harsh "Hah!"

I looked at Abuela. "She did, didn't she?"

Abuela sighed, "She did."

"Is that why she left me here?"

Abuela wouldn't look at me when she softly said, "Martha, she would have used any reasoning, any justification to leave you here."

I sat back in my chair. My throat felt tight and my stomach ached like someone had punched me. They continued bickering.

"I still don't think this is a . . . "

"¡Ya, Gloria! Don't start . . . "

My mother knew about my gift. She could have left me here because of the gift . . . No . . . that wasn't true. She jumped out of a window. If she truly left me here for the gift, she could have just said that. She left me because she just didn't want me. Oddly, I couldn't help but wish my mother was here to confirm it.

But this apprenticeship . . . learning the things that my grandmother did in her back room? Part of me felt like arguing with Abuela. Maybe I didn't want to be a *curandera*. I mean, who was *she* to say what I was going to do or not do? And maybe I *didn't* have the gift—Abuela could be wrong. Part of me knew that was a lie; I'd never felt like I had earlier, helping Señora Flores and Señor Díaz. It was exhilarating. I felt like I was good at something beyond drawing.

God, Laura was going to die when she heard about this. Oh, shit, and Marcela. She'd go crazy when she found out. Then again, it'd serve her right. What I saw today . . . No wonder Abuela didn't take Marcela as an apprentice. Marcela speaking to leaves? Yeah, right.

My thoughts boiled as I listened to Abuela and Gloria speak about me as if I wasn't there. Gloria telling Abuela how ridiculous this was, Abuela telling her to shut her mouth. They didn't even care about my thoughts, and this was all about me!

"Doesn't anyone want to know what I want?"

Gloria and my grandmother stopped speaking and looked at me with the same expression: eyes opened wide, nostrils flared and lips pursed.

Guess not.

Seis

"UM, JUANITA, can I ask you something?" I said.

Juanita sat in the front room. The rest of the family was in the living room, doing impressions of the bishop who had visited our church that morning. He had spoken with a lisp, stuttered over his words and even said "Omen" instead of "Amen." Even though there were fewer people this Sunday at my cousin Carlos' house—a few of the families were in San Antonio visiting relatives—the regular noise level was being maintained. In front of me, Juanita was tickling Lilia on her lap.

She set her down on the floor and patted her back to go and play, which was all the encouragement Lilia needed. Lilia stuck her tongue out playfully at me as she ran to the living room where the other children were.

"Hola, Martha. How've you been? How's school?"

I sat down on the couch next to her. "School's great. Actually, the other day I ran across this picture of my mother as homecoming queen."

Juanita's face dropped at the mention of my mother, but she quickly resumed a nonchalant look.

"Yes, Rosa was the homecoming queen her junior year. She loved being the queen."

"I'm sure. She looked a little different in the picture, too."

"Ever the pretty one."

Okay, this wasn't going well. I didn't want to piss Juanita off by bringing up old jealousies. *Get to the point, Martha.*

"There was a girl and a guy in the picture. Carlita and Jorge? Were they all friends?"

"Carlita Juárez and Jorge Valdez? I haven't heard those names in a while. What made you think they were friends with Rosa?" Her eyes regarded me suspiciously.

"They had their arms around each other, were laughing. They just looked like friends."

Juanita didn't buy it yet. Her lips had set into the famous Gonzalez woman line of suspicion. I had to come up with something else.

I looked down at my hands and traced the lines on my left palm so Juanita wouldn't see my face. "I only want to know my mother a little better. It helped, seeing that photograph. I miss her so much, and I don't know . . . it just helped. I felt connected to her. I know that sounds stupid."

"Oh, Martha, don't say that."

I looked up. A string of emotions crossed her face: concern, pity and finally belief. I tried not to smile at my victory.

"Carlita and Rosa were best friends and Jorge and Rosa dated for a year or so. They were a crazy lot, always running around, giving Mamá headaches all the time."

I laughed at that and Juanita did too, breaking the tension. This was as perfect a moment as it would get.

"So, do they still live here? In Laredo, I mean?"

"You know, I think they moved." She stood up. "I'm going to go see if Mamá and Gloria need help in the kitchen." And she walked away without another word.

I had my answer. They were still here.

After finding my cousin Carlos alone, I asked him if he had a phone book. Abuela sure didn't—hell, we barely used the phone, usually only when someone called with an emergency. Thankfully, Carlos did, and what's more it was in the drawer of his bedside table and not in the family room or in the kitchen where Abuela or Gloria might see me. He showed me where it was, then left me to join the rest of the family.

I turned to 'J' only to find a thousand Juárezes. It was the same for Valdez, although Valdez was shorter by a few names or so. There were four Carlita Juárezes and seven Jorge Valdezes. Some had addresses, while others only had numbers. A few had both. I wrote down each number and address with a pen and a piece of paper from a small notepad I found in a drawer. I wouldn't be able to call any of these numbers soon; it might take weeks.

When I left the room, I stuffed the papers in the only place I could hide them: my bra. There were no pockets in the horrendously flowery Sunday dress Abuela had made me wear. As I left the bedroom, I bumped into Gloria, who was heading to the bathroom.

"What were you doing in there?"

I put my hands to my breast, feeling the paper beneath the fabric.

"Praying."

I returned home on Monday after school to find my grandmother sitting in the kitchen, strumming her fingers on the table, staring at the entryway.

"What took so long?" she asked and then stood up.

"It's the same time I usually get home." I flung my backpack in the chair that she had just gotten up from and sat down myself.

"Don't sit. Come. You learn today."

"But I have a lot of homework."

"After." She waddled into the hallway.

"But, you know, I . . . "

"¡*Vámonos!*"

When I entered the hallway, Abuela stood at the mystery door, the one she went into to do her healing work. She pulled out a key from her pants' pocket and stuck it into the lock.

Abuela opened the door and walked in. I moved forward and stopped just before the door. I was reminded of the first day I had walked into Abuela's canary yellow kitchen. That feeling of what would come, of change, of the unknown, of rejection, all of those feelings returned now. I pushed my hair from my face and felt a nervous sweat on the back of my neck.

When I crossed the threshold into my grandmother's secret room, I would be crossing over into the world of *curanderismo*, and it would forever change my life. But I had to do this. I wanted to, maybe. I took a deep breath and stepped through. I had survived Laredo so far.

Drying herbs hung from the ceiling like the limbs of drooping trees. Some hung so low I had to be wary not to hit them with my head. I was taller than my grandmother, and she must have hung them so as to not hit *her* head. They made the room smell divine, like sweet, wet earth and lavender, so I couldn't complain. With each breath, I felt calmer. My grandmother had walked across the room to what looked like a small altar on the far wall. She knelt down slowly as I walked to her.

In the center of the room was a long, wooden table standing two feet off the floor covered with a brightly stitched yellow and red zigzag pad. Woven blankets, like the ones I slept under, were folded at the end of the table, and a small stool sat next to it. Hanging on the walls were old, wooden shelves. Some shelves were filled with pans and pots, others with jars. I couldn't tell what was in the jars, only that some looked like powder, while other jars held actual objects that I was unable to recognize from so far away. Small paintings of angels and Jesus printed on tiny cards stood between the items on the shelves.

Despite everything, the room was organized and clean. The rest of the house was cluttered and chaotic compared to this. When I got to the altar, I knelt down beside my grandmother and sat back on my calves as she did. I wasn't sure what else to do. Do as the *curanderas* do, right?

The altar was a small wooden table covered in a white cloth that had different colored embroidery with looping, flowery designs on the edges. The fabric looked old, slightly yellowed. A larger ceramic statue of the Virgin Mary holding a baby Jesus stood in the center. A cross made of dried, yellowish leaves leaned against it. Surrounding Mary and Jesus were the holy troops, saints and angels, hands folded in prayer looking up at Mother and Son in holy reverence. Next to the statues was a bundle of sage that gave off a strong yet soothing odor.

Small picture frames littered the table. Photos of my mother when she was younger, Juanita and her family, even a sepia picture of my grandfather in his army uniform. He looked to be in his twenties. Small knickknacks of pouches, rocks and dried flowers also decorated the altar, but I wasn't aware of their significance, and they didn't seem to be placed in any particular order.

I felt nervous, like I was going to accidentally hit something and then ruin the entire ambience of the room. Keeping my elbows close to my body, I turned to Abuela. She waited impatiently. Not that she said anything, but I had become accustomed to noticing the pursing of the lips, the tight way in which she held herself.

"Okay, we pray first." Abuela closed her eyes and interlaced her hands in her lap.

"Why?" I whispered. There was an essence about the room that didn't want to be disturbed. It felt wrong to speak normally, so I whispered.

She took a deep breath of patience. Maybe she was nervous too. "We must ask *Dios* to forgive us of our sins so that He may give us strength and guidance. A *curandera* is nothing without *Dios*. *Dios* gives us our gift to heal."

"Oh. So do we say it aloud or to ourselves . . . ?"

"Have you ever prayed?"

I averted my eyes. If I wasn't godly enough, could I still be a *curandera*?

"What do you do at church?" she asked.

I shrugged. "I don't know . . . at first I just looked at everything, you know, the paintings, the statues, the candles and all . . . Or keep up with all the sitting and kneeling. Now I just try to translate all the words the priest says."

"That's not bad, exactly. But church is more than statues and words. It is *Dios y Cristo y María*. You must believe if you are to maintain your *don*."

Believe? A little easier said than done. "What's a *don*?"

"I will explain later. Here. We will pray together."

She grabbed my hands and held them between us. This was a different side of my grandmother: a dedicated woman who put aside her toughness for focus and serenity. I closed my eyes before she began.

She said the prayer aloud: "*Dios*, forgive us of our sins. You have given us the gift to heal and we are humble to this gift. Open up the soul of my granddaughter to you, her ears to my learning and her body to the power of healing," she paused. "And please give me the strength and knowledge to teach the daughter of my daughter. Amen."

I followed with an "Amen" of my own and opened my eyes.

Abuela sighed. She let go of my hands, pushed herself to a standing position and went near the door. I followed and stood next to her so that we faced the room.

"Now we start," she said.

"Start how?"

She motioned with her hand to the room. "You will learn everything in this room. Everything has a purpose in here, and you will learn it. You will learn the material and the spiritual."

"What does that mean?"

"May I have a chance to explain without you interrupting?"

She waited for a sarcastic response, but I refused to ruin this. I didn't want us arguing when she could be telling me things.

"Material, *nieta,* is what Señor Díaz and Señora Flores do. They make teas and pastes, use herbs, give massages, sweat cleanses—physical healings. They heal with the earth and with physical labor. But spiritual is more than that. It's healing on a different plane. *And* there's mental healing."

"And?"

"And what?"

"And I still don't really understand what you mean about spiritual and now mental. You didn't really tell me anything."

"Impatience will not help you to be a *curandera*. Besides, you must learn the physical before the spiritual and the mental."

She stepped forward to one of the shelves on the right side of the room.

"Wait," I said.

She stopped and looked back at me.

"I don't know if I can do this. I've never done magic or anything. Maybe you are wrong about my gift."

"Like I told you yesterday, I've known you've had the gift since the first day you arrived. And I'm never wrong." She smiled. Then suddenly, her voice was hard and serious, "And we don't do magic, only *brujas* do. Magic. Bah!"

Abuela grabbed a stool next to one of the shelves, climbed up and handed me a few jars. I placed them on the counter beneath the shelves.

The first one I recognized before she even opened the jar. "Garlic," I said.

"Yes, *para* bowel pains, toothaches and stomach troubles." She grabbed a second jar. "And this one?"

I shrugged. It looked like a bunch of leaves to me.

"*Éste es alcanfor*, camphor."

I took a step forward and peered into the jar. The jar smelled like moth balls. The leaves were glossy, yet waxy-looking, and a few black-colored berries were sprinkled among the leaves.

"It helps with pain. Like headaches and rheumatism, even with faintness. Now this next one . . . "

"How?" I said.

"How what?"

"Well, how does camphor help with pain? Do you drink it or touch it? How does it cure those things?"

"It depends. Right now you only need to know what they treat."

"Shouldn't I learn how to treat something at the same time?"

Abuela jammed the lid back on the jar, even though it was one of those lids that needed to be twisted on. "Forgive me, almighty *curandera*. I forgot you know best."

"No. Sorry. Okay, just go ahead. I'll listen."

She pursed her lips and grabbed another jar. "Aster, for coughs and congestion of the chest." Then another one, "Amaranth, *para el corazón*, for heart trouble."

An idea hit me. Crap, she wasn't going to like me interrupting, but this was a good reason.

"Hold on, before you continue."

Abuela threw her hands in the air, "*Ay, m'ija, ¿ahora qué?*"

"This is only the third jar and it's a lot of new words I've never heard of. Can I get a notepad or something to write it all down, maybe make a few sketches of the plants, to study?" I smiled.

"*¿Pluma y papel? ¡Ay!* My grandmother handed down this information from her mother before her and her mother before her and not with any fancy pen and paper."

"But it will take me weeks to memorize all this . . . without paper!"

"That's how you will learn. No more questions."

"Pen and paper isn't even fancy. They have computers these days."

"*¡Bah! ¡Tecnología!*" she said and climbed on the stool to bring down more jars. Even though I was a bit annoyed that Abuela wouldn't let me write everything down, I smiled to myself. She had called me "*mi'ja.*"

For the next few hours, my grandmother pulled out many jars filled with spices, oils, dried fruit, dried leaves, stems from plants and even jars filled with dead animals or animal parts that smelt so bad that I gagged a few times. She opened each jar and let me smell and even touch its contents. I was repulsed touching the dead animals. A lot of the leaves looked *so* similar. How would I be able to tell them apart?

So much information! It felt like thousands of hands pushed on my brain, but there just wasn't enough room. How could there be all this knowledge? And if these things did what she said they could, then why were there even doctors? But now I understood a little of why Marcela wanted to be an apprentice. If I learned all this stuff that my grandmother was showing me, I would have some power. I would be special, more so than the average person, and I supposed that was the appeal of *curanderismo.*

It was impossible to remember everything she told me that day, and it would take a while to remember how everything was used, thanks to Abuela's "traditional ways." Although, I won't lie, that night I found some empty pages in a spiral and tried to write down as much information as I could remember, with a few drawings of the plants here and there. It was pretty difficult to do, since there was so much to fit into my mind: ingredients with weird names, leaves and stems with funny, little details.

We only got through half the jars that night and, when we returned to the kitchen, Gloria was already there cooking a meal of *huevos con nopales*. I didn't realize I was starving until I smelled the food.

I didn't fully believe the magical mumbo jumbo, but something about it was enjoyable. Abuela and I were connecting, sort of, and I was learning something that other people didn't learn. I smiled throughout the meal, shrugging off all of Gloria's sarcastic remarks.

I wasn't even reprimanded for it.

The rest of the week transformed into a new routine that I would maintain for many months: enter the healing room, pray and then learn about Abuela's tools, objects, herbs and plants. I learned how to use incense and candles, that certain colors healed certain things. I memorized plant abilities, which herbs cured what and how to squeeze precious juice from the roots of a plant. I practiced with different tools, using certain knives to cut leaves and other knives that made slicing and dicing dead animals easier. I learned that religious objects were for more than decoration, and even discovered that a pouch that hung on the wall was protection against evil spirits, that a broom swept away *malo* and other forms of evil.

The most important thing I learned was basically meditation, although my grandmother didn't call it that. She called it *reflexión*, but the process was much the same, except for one particular thing.

"Why are we doing this?" I said as I opened one of my eyes to peek at Abuela.

We sat with our legs crossed in front of the altar, facing one another, our hands turned down flat on our knees. My lower back ached after five minutes of sitting, and I kept squirming to get comfortable. Abuela sat straight-backed and did not appear to be in any state of discomfort.

She kept her eyes closed. "You have an extra healing gift that others do not. Your *don*, the place within you where your gift comes from, is spiritual and mental. When you learn your body, you will find your gift."

"So this *don* will do all the healing for me?"

"No, you heal through your *don*," she said.

"So, how would I know if I'm using my *don* or not?"

Abuela laughed. "Oh, trust me, you will know. It's like nothing you've ever felt before."

"How am I learning my body by sitting here with my eyes closed?"

"*¡Ay, muchacha!* Can you ever be quiet? Stop talking and breathe in and out. Allow yourself to leave your body. Only then will you be able to see your *don*."

I stuck out my tongue in annoyance.

"I saw that."

I opened my right eye, but Abuela's eyes were shut. I closed my eye.

"Saw what?"

"I saw what you did. With my *don*."

I opened my right eye again and stuck my tongue out once more.

"I saw that, too." Her eyes were closed the entire time.

I closed my eyes, maybe a little more of a believer in this whole *don* thing.

That Saturday, Abuela resumed her rounds helping the sick in the neighborhood. Instead of sitting in the kitchens of the homes she visited, I now went into the rooms with her and her patients. I assumed what Abuela did was like a typical doctor's visit, but I didn't remember myself ever being sick or visiting a doctor. I asked Abuela if that was normal.

She nodded. "Your *don* and your age protected you from most illnesses. Besides that, you just got lucky."

When Abuela entered the room where the sick person was, her entire mood changed: a load was lifted, she smiled more, laughed at times, and her voice did not hold the toughness it usually did. Her mood was infectious, so that I found myself smiling goofily as I watched her interact with the sick.

Usually, my grandmother swept the room with sage that she pulled out of her bag and then proceeded to hold the patient's hand and pray with him or her. After that, she would immediately begin her healing by telling the patient what needed to be done to cure the sickness. At first, I believed she had been previously told the person's sickness, until once an old woman said, "How did you know that I had migraines? I never told you, did I?"

My grandmother only smiled and repeated the instructions for the tea that would help relieve the pain. As soon as we left a house, I began with the same question.

"How did you know? Have any of these people that we've seen told you what was wrong with them?"

"Yes, some have told me."

I walked faster in front of her to be able to see her face. "But did they need to tell you? Or did you already know?"

Abuela's face had lost the light-heartedness that it had held minutes earlier, so that now she looked annoyed at me. "Of course, I already knew. With my *don* I saw what was wrong."

"What do you mean by you 'saw' what was wrong?"

"Saw, see. With my eyes. I thought you were smart." She nudged my shoulder.

"I am! But you're telling me something that sounds crazy. You make it sound like I will be able to see the disease."

She nodded. "Yes, that is exactly it."

"I don't know if I buy it. What does disease even look like?"

"Dark and ugly."

Figures. "So if this is real, how do I make it happen?"

"With your *don*."

"I know that, but how?"

She stopped and looked at me. "By not complaining during *reflexión*, by trying to find your *don* inside you . . . and by believing."

I silently vowed to never complain about *reflexión* again. Although Abuela said this *don* stuff wasn't magic, it sure sounded that way to me, and I wanted to experience it myself.

Still, watching my grandmother work on patients was another experience entirely. I had started to become comfortable in the culturally unique world of Laredo. Perhaps it was because I had learned Spanish so rapidly and it linked me to everything. But after witnessing the different ways in which my grandmother cured illnesses, I was thrown seven steps back from what I thought I had gained in understanding the Mexican culture.

She used eggs to massage the arthritic joints of her ailing patients. She spat on the chest of children to rid them of whooping cough. She gave a woman a dried hummingbird as a love charm. She threw holy water in the shape of a cross on the bodies of dying patients and knelt, praying for hours, sometimes aloud, and then she'd place her hands on the parts of their body that were failing and pray to God to heal them. She cured someone of fright—*susto*—yes, fright! As if someone could get sick by being scared? I gained a whole new set of vocabulary words that dealt with illnesses that weren't illnesses at all. *Susto, mal de ojo, nerviosismo* . . . illnesses caused by fright so that the soul became lost, illnesses caused by people looking at you with jealousy, illnesses caused by nervousness. We were not supposed to just cure the physical ailments of someone's body but their mental state, too!

It sounded like something a psychologist or a mental hospital should cure. How could someone get sick by being scared? Abuela tried to explain that it was the *soul* we were curing. And yet, that scared me more. She wanted *me* to cure a soul? That was a lot of responsibility. I listened more carefully when she explained the spiritual illnesses because I never wanted anyone to come back and say I had ruined their soul.

"And sometimes they aren't cured," Abuela also told me.

"So, what's the point of all this if we don't actually cure them every time?"

"Do the *gringo* doctors cure their patients of everything, every time?"

She had a point. Abuela explained it was give and take in the world, and mostly God's will, and how much the person believed in what we did or if they wanted to be healed.

I was still an outsider to the whole religious aspect of *curanderismo*—the God part. I did not understand something I had no attachment to yet. Although Abuela pushed me to "feel God" and "hear God," you can't force someone until they are ready to touch and listen.

It took time, and day by day, the things I saw and experienced started to become more normal to me, started to make sense.

A few weeks into my apprenticeship, Marcela and her friends marched up to me in the hallway on my way to class.

"Hey, *puta*, I heard you have a new job."

Instead of stopping, I kept walking, so she had to walk faster to keep up with me.

"You hear a lot of things about me, Marcela. Some would call it an obsession."

Everyone stopped in the hallway and stared at us as we walked by. Suddenly, Marcela sprinted ahead of me and cut me off.

"What do you want? I need to get to class," I said.

Marcela's eyes darkened with anger, and the vein on her forehead pulsed faster. "I asked you a question. Are you apprenticing to your damn grandmother?'

I don't know if I was tired from all the extra work Abuela had given me, or if I was just tired of Marcela speaking to me like that and cursing my grandmother, but I let her get to me.

"Yes! What does it matter?"

"You told me you weren't her apprentice." Her face reddened beneath her pale make-up.

"I wasn't then, but I am now. And I'm tired of you being pissed off because Abuela turned you away." As soon as I said the words, I felt so much truth in them. But I wanted those words back in my mouth because I knew right away that I had pissed her off more than ever.

Marcela pulled a fist back, ready to take a punch at the same time that I made my hands into fists.

It was then that a ninth-grade science teacher spoke up. "Is there a problem here?"

The teacher stood by her door on the opposite side of the hallway, staring at us. Everyone around us became quiet, tensed for something to happen. I returned my focus back to Marcela. I saw it: she hated me with so much passion she could barely contain it.

One of her thug friends moved between us, gave me a cold stare and said in a low voice, "Come on, Marcela. You know you can't get expelled again."

I looked at the teacher and said, "We're fine, Mrs. . . ." I looked past her at the sign next to her door. "Mrs. Gómez. Everything is fine."

I turned back around to see that Marcela had moved closer to me while her friend had moved to the side. She was so close that I saw the lines between the shades of grey and black eye shadow she had applied that morning.

Marcela spoke low so that not even her friend could hear. "Talk to me like that again, little girl, and you're going to feel my steel in your gut."

She patted her jean pocket, where something stretched against the fabric. My first thought went to the rumor Laura had told me when I first moved here, of the girl that Marcela had almost stabbed to death. First fear shot through me, then anger.

"No, you listen to me. Leave me alone. With the stuff I'm learning from Abuela, your 'steel' can't hurt me."

It was a lie. I knew it before the words were coming out, but she didn't know that. Marcela wanted something stronger than steel, something that would bring fear just by saying the name. I only knew the basic healing properties of herbs. I didn't know curses, or spells, or any *mal* that could hurt others, but I wanted Marcela to think I did. I knew she'd believe it, because that is what she wanted. Power. Control.

Her eyes widened a bit, and she stepped back. Not exactly in fear, but in awe, or perhaps desire. She wanted to be my grandmother's apprentice. Wanted the knowledge of *curanderas* but for all the wrong reasons.

I walked past her and headed to class.

Sunday, at another *primo*'s house after church, I snuck into the bedroom and called the list of Jorge Valdezeses first. While some numbers were disconnected, a few Jorges answered. It wasn't until the sixth number I called that I had some kind of luck. The man who answered wasn't Jorge, but his cousin, Felipe. He said my mother's name sounded familiar, maybe Jorge knew my mother and maybe he didn't. He gave me the address of Jorge's job, Gutierrez Body Shop. He said I would find Jorge there seven days a week. I thanked him and hung up. Unfortunately, I wasn't able to call any of the Carlitas because a few of my little cousins found me in the bedroom and dragged me out to the front yard to push them on an old, wooden swing.

The next day, when the bell had rung for school to be let out, I asked Laura if she knew where the Gutierrez Body Shop was. She shifted her book bag to her other shoulder and grabbed the paper I had with Jorge's name and the name of the garage.

"Yeah, I know it. It's down the street from the down-town market, where my mom's shop is."

"Shop?"

"My mom owns a boutique called Sofía's Cosa's. She sells nickknacks, jewelry, clothes, house stuff."

Laura gave me directions from the school to the garage. The downtown market was the same one that Abuela had taken me to on the first weekend I had arrived in Laredo. It wasn't that far from the house, so the garage would be within walking distance, too.

Before Laura gave me the piece of paper back she pulled it closer to her face and squinted. "Valdez?" She looked up at me.

I grabbed the paper from her. "Just someone I need to talk to. Why?"

"I'm a Valdez."

I fumbled with one of my textbooks and then caught it. She was right. I vaguely remember her telling me her last name was Valdez when we first met. God, I was stu-pid.

"Do you know a Jorge Valdez?"

She shook her head no. "Sorry, I don't even know my own dad."

"Is Valdez his last name?"

"Yeah, my mom gave it to me, but she won't even tell me his first name. Says he died long ago, so there's no reason I should know about him."

"Sounds like something Abuela would say."

Laura giggled. "Well, good luck with finding the guy. Why do you need to talk to him?"

I wasn't going to have that conversation. "Sorry, I gotta get home. Abuela will kill me if I'm five minutes late." I waved and started to turn away.

"Martha, wait." Laura looked behind her, then to her side. She walked closer to me and spoke low. "Look, if you get a chance, come by my mom's shop sometime on a Saturday. I work there on the weekends."

"You know if Abuela found out, I'd be dead."

Laura's eyes darted back and forth. "I know, but this is important. I have to show you something. My mom works in the back doing inventory on Saturdays, so she wouldn't even see you."

"Maybe. I don't know. I could tr . . . "

"Okay, good." Laura smiled. "I'll see you soon, okay? Soon." She gave me one last stare before turning around and walking off.

That was weird. I headed for the Pepto Bismol house. I didn't really have time to think about Laura's request. I had more important things on my mind. Like how I was going to actually go to the garage, since my grandmother was always at home, and with my *curandera* apprenticeship, I barely had time to finish school work at night. More patience? It was almost the end of October. As soon as I found out where my mother was, I was going to flip out on her for making me go through all this work.

A few days later, I returned home to find the Cadillac missing and the house empty. I was more of a believer in God at that moment than ever before. There was a note on the kitchen table written in English. It said that my grandmother had been called to an emergency on the opposite side of the border and that she would return home late. There were leftovers in the fridge. It was signed by Gloria with the following written beneath her name: "P.S. Act right, *chica*."

I didn't waste a second thinking about what I was about to do. I dropped my backpack and rushed out the front door. It was a twenty-five-minute walk to the garage and I didn't know how long it would take to talk to the guy. Besides, I wanted to return as quickly as possible, just in case Abuela returned early.

I practically ran to the garage and got there in fifteen minutes, sweating. Even though it was October, it was still hot. The garage, a rusted gray building that looked ready to topple over, stood on a corner. Cars, some fairly old, yet with new paint jobs and new accessories, stood in between newer, broken-down cars with missing or rusted parts in the front drive of the garage and in the street. A large garage door stood open on the left side. Three guys worked on a red Chevy with the hood popped open while another watched.

This was it. Would he be here? Would he be the right Jorge Valdez, or was he lost and my mother with him? I didn't have long to think or be nervous. Abuela was going to come home whether I got my answers or not. I walked to the open garage door. Before I was even fifteen feet from it, the man who had been watching the three guys work noticed me.

"Can I help you?" he asked.

My mouth became dry. He looked down at me over his bushy, grey mustache.

"*Sí*, uh, does a Jorge Valdez work here?" I asked.

The man regarded me for a second, debating whether or not to tell me. Then he motioned with his head to the right. A lone man worked under the hood of a cream-colored car on the other side of the garage.

"*Gracias.*" I felt the old man's eyes watching me as I walked away. Now that I was in the garage, the over-

whelming stench of oil and grease and the heavy, rubber
smell of tires assaulted me. Instead of pulling my shirt
over my nose like I wanted to, I focused on my target.

The man known as Jorge Valdez was hidden in the
depths of the car's opened hood. I wasn't sure if it was
him. The man wore a white tank with faded blue jeans
that had oil and grime marks down the sides of them, as
if he wiped his hands on them every few seconds. His
arms were a tanned brown and a little on the meaty side.
His stomach rolled over the edge of his jeans, even more
so since he was bent over.

As I walked up, Led Zeppelin's "Black Dog" rang out.
No way. Rock in Laredo? I couldn't contain myself.

"Is Zeppelin *actually* on the radio?"

The man stood up and turned to me, holding a screwdriver. It was him, the Jorge Valdez I was looking for.
Even after all those years, the youthful teenager shone
out from the hardened lines of his face. His deep
widow's peak looked more pronounced with the straight,
black, hair that fell around his face. A thick, black mustache coated his upper lip now, but damn it, it was Jorge.

He looked at me, his head cocked to the side. "You
like Zeppelin?"

"Yeah. But I didn't know anyone else down here did.
I've only heard Tejano and cumbias and stuff."

Smiling, Jorge placed the screwdriver in his front
pocket and grabbed a towel hanging on the hood. He
leaned casually against the truck as he wiped his hands.

"There's a few of us down here who like rock. A
group of us even get together and play, but we don't get
many gigs," he said.

I smiled. And he played in a *band*? My mom's cup of
tea.

Then he asked, "How old are you, kid?"

"Sixteen."

"Don't know many sixteen-year-olds who like bands like Zeppelin. You guys are usually into that punk stuff."

I didn't know how to respond, so I just shrugged.

My mother had dated a guy once, Bob, who had worked for a rock & roll radio station. Each time she took me to the station, he'd introduce me to a new album of a different band: Zeppelin, Pink Floyd, Aerosmith, The Beatles, Jimi Hendrix and the list went on. Bob was the only guy who had ever paid me much attention.

"So is that on the radio?" I asked.

He laughed, and it was his laugh that made me see why my mother had fallen for him. He was pretty hand-some even for an old guy. "No, that's a tape a cousin from Austin sent me."

I replied with, "Cool," just as he finished wiping his hands.

"So you come to the garage to just talk rock or can I help you with something?"

"Uh, yes, I think so. My name is Martha George. I've been looking for you."

"Need a semi-good band for a gig?" he joked.

I took a second and licked my dry lips. "My mother is Rosa Gonzalez."

As soon as her name hit the air, his shoulders stiff-ened for a second. His feet shuffled away from the car while he looked behind me as if expecting her to be there in the shadows. He was not the joking, relaxed guy he had been a moment ago. Jorge was on edge, a scared animal backed in a corner.

"Sorry, but I don't know who you're talking about."

"Yes, you do. You used to be her boyfriend in high school," I said.

He laughed mockingly. "Look there were a lot of Rosa Gonzalezes at my school. And I had a lot of girlfriends."

My face burned. "I only need a few answers, and then I'll leave. I just want to know if you've seen or talked to her within the last few months."

His mouth was set in a grim line, and his dark eyes looked at me with such anger. It was as if I was uncovering something he had tried to forget. What had just happened? One moment we were talking rock, he was being cool, and now he was lying to me. We stared at each other, neither one wanting to blink first. The chorus played and I caught the lyrics, *Eyes that shine burning red . . .*

"I don't know who . . . " he began.

"That's bullshit. I know you know her. I saw homecoming pictures of you two at school. I know it's you."

He shuffled his feet some more and shook his head, looking like a mad child. "I haven't seen your mother since high school."

"Do you at least know why she left in the first place? What happened?"

"If you want to know why she left, ask her!" He turned away from me, but I stopped his movement short with my next words.

"If I knew where she was, I'd ask her. The only people who might tell me something I want to know are you and Carlita Juárez. And since I found you first, I'm here."

His body slumped, and his arms hung at his sides. He refused to look at me. "Leave things in the past. Move on. Your mother did."

My fists clenched at my side. "Thanks for the advice, *cabrón*. At least tell me where I can find Carlita Juárez."

Jorge looked inside the front hood. "I don't know anyone by that name."

Whatever had happened with my mother had been big. It had to be. Jorge wanted to keep the secret just as much as Abuela and everyone else in my family did. But why? I didn't know if he knew how to contact Carlita or not, but fuck it—this *pendejo* wasn't going to help me. And to think, for a moment there I had thought he was cool. I turned around to leave.

"Don't come back here," he said softly.

"Gladly!" I yelled as I stomped past the other workers and the old man with the bushy mustache.

When Abuela returned home that night, I was already in bed. She opened the door and looked in on me, but my body was wrapped in blankets, turned away from her. I stared at the wall with so much anger that I'm surprised the crucifixes didn't fall off and clatter to the floor.

Siete

ABOUT A WEEK after I had found Jorge Valdez, I returned home from school to find my grandmother waiting for me on the porch, her short, chunky arms crossed over a pale, pink sleeveless top and her lips pursed in anger.

I almost stopped when I saw her. What was she upset about now?

"*Buenas tardes,* Abuela."

"You've been going behind my back? Keeping secrets in my house?"

I stopped. The sun beat down on my head and I fought the need to look down or anywhere from her squinting eyes.

Keep your cool. "What are you talking about?" I walked up the steps to escape into the shadow of the house.

She walked to me as I opened the screen door. I had to escape her, keep the guilt from showing on my face.

"Threats to my granddaughter? *¿Mi nieta?* And you threatening back?"

Marcela. Thank God. I walked to the kitchen to grab some cold water from the pitcher in the fridge.

"Abuela, it was nothing really . . . " She cut me off.

"*¿Nada? ¡¿Nada?!* That little girl causing trouble for my granddaughter! I won't allow it."

Hearing Abuela speak with so much passion and protection for me made me smile. My mother had *never* done that.

"Stop that smiling. Turn around."

God, how did she do that? I turned around, trying to wipe the smile from my face with little success.

She got closer and pointed her finger up at me. "*Nunca*, never, never threaten someone with your gifts. Do you hear me? I won't be having a *brujita* in my family. *Curanderismo* is good. Evil intentions, even evil thoughts, won't be tolerated. And stay away from that girl. Don't speak to her, and tell me if she bothers you again. *¿Me entiendes?* Do you understand?"

I nodded. It was best not to say a word. She snatched away the pitcher of water and the cup I had in my hand and ushered me into her *curandera* room for two hours of *reflexión*.

I still had Carlita to rely on for answers about my mother, since Jorge had refused to help me. At least I hoped I did. The only problem was that I had a list of Carlitas, some with numbers and some without. I didn't even want to think about the fact that she might be listed under a married name.

Each Sunday, I snuck into a family member's room to use their telephone. Sometimes I got in two calls, sometimes only one, before I had to sneak back out into the family area so Abuela and Gloria wouldn't discover that I was missing. It took six Sundays to make it all the way through the numbers without any luck. It appeared that my only chance of finding the Carlita I searched for would be to go to the addresses listed without numbers, which sucked. How was I actually going to go to the houses without my grandmother knowing? I got lucky that one time with Jorge. When would the next unexpected emergency appear and help me?

Despite the fact that it looked hopeless, I had to stay positive. And patient, which was worse than staying positive, because I had to know. I just had to. I had found out so much already, so much in fact that I felt as if I would die if I didn't ever find out the whole truth.

I decided to map the houses, regardless of whether I would ever actually have a chance to go to them. There were three street addresses. I asked Laura if she recognized any of the street names. She recognized one, said it was a few blocks from the Pepto Bismol house, but the other two streets she didn't recognize. I went to the school's library and found a map of the city. One house was located three streets over, another was four blocks away, and one was located on the other side of the city. I prayed Carlita was in one of the three because without Carlita, I'd be stuck.

No Carlita equaled no mother, and no answers.

One Sunday we were at my *primo* Lolo's house. The kitchen had a revolving door that had to be pushed in or out. Abuela, a few *tías* and a few cousins were in the kitchen cooking. I was thirsting for Kool-Aid, and I had barely pushed open the door, when I heard my name.

"You still teaching Martha that witch stuff, María?" Tía Julia said.

Before my grandmother responded, Gloria did. "Julia, how dare you! María heals your kids and has treated your husband all these years for that *cochino* disease, and you can still call her a *bruja*?"

"María isn't supposed to tell you that!" Tía Julia said.

"Ah, bah! Everyone knows where your husband goes every night. From now on, tell him to go to one of those fake healers with their stores, and see how much they steal from you!"

My cousin Sonia tried to steer the conversation to less violent waters. "I heard Martha is learning a lot. To have a gift is such a blessing."

Others murmured their agreement. Abuela remained quiet.

Laura's older cousin, Tierra, who happened to show up at this family gathering spoke next: "Laura tells me that Martha's enjoying it—and doing well in school, too."

A loud bang echoed after Laura's name was spoken, followed by Gloria saying, "Can no one keep their mouth shut today?"

Which reminded me. I still hadn't gone to Laura's mother's store to find out what Laura needed to tell me.

"As long as Martha stays away from the *pachucos*, she will have no problem," some other cousin commented.

My tía Elsa spoke next. "Speaking of Martha, I saw that boy that Rosa dated in high school the other day. He remembered me. Works at an auto shop fixing cars and . . . "

My heart pounded harder. I released my hands on the door a little, in case someone looked my way and noticed the open door. Did that *cabrón* tell Elsa that I had stopped by his shop? She couldn't keep her big mouth shut to save her own children.

Elsa continued speaking. "He had some child with him. She was so disrespectful! What's wrong with these parents in Laredo? Raising God-less kids. Thank goodness Rosa and he broke up, I mean if . . . "

"Elsa!" Gloria shouted with an edge to her voice. "*Cá-llate*, already! Hurry and finish the *frijoles*. Chatting away like we don't have a thousand Mexican mouths waiting to be fed!"

I wished that I had seen Abuela's face. I wished Gloria hadn't been there. I only had the outer pieces of the puzzle, and someone or something was always keeping me from obtaining the ones that would put it all together.

Even though my family was intent on keeping something from me, I didn't act any differently with Abuela. Actually, we were closer than ever as I continued to learn all the healing arts and discover my gifts.

Señor Peña had come to Abuela for help with kidney stones. It had taken many visits to convince him to let me work on him. It wasn't that he didn't like me, it was just that many of Abuela's patients didn't trust me to heal them . . . yet. I was young in their eyes, and they only trusted my grandmother's gifts.

"She heals you or you go to the doctor. Your choice," Abuela told Señor Peña.

He chewed on his bottom lip, placed his bony hands on his hips and looked me up and down, which kind of pissed me off. I crossed my arms and stared back.

After a moment, he looked down and gave a sharp nod. He chose me over the doctor.

The doctor was three things in Laredo: expensive, white and sometimes the devil. Señor Peña was part of the older generation, and people like him were used to *curanderas*, natural healings. Doctors, pills and surgeries were not for people like him. Some from the older generation fell for the commercialized *curanderas* that had set up shops on Saunders Street and McPherson Street.

Many lost their money and their hope, only to return to Abuela later with apologies for trying out something new.

I looked at Abuela, and she gave me a nod to go ahead. I had the floor.

"Would you please lie down, Señor Peña?" I motioned at the table.

He shrugged his bony shoulders toward his droopy ears. "If you say so."

I got a whiff of bacon as he was laying down. He fidgeted on the table and watched me as I knelt down beside him.

Without waiting, I began a prayer: "*Dios*, please guide me in this healing. Through you I can do all things and through your guidance I can rid your son of his pain. Amen."

"Is that it?"

Through gritted teeth, I said, "Yes."

His eyes were closed, but his brows rose as if he was surprised. "Amen, then."

Oh, I was fighting the frustration. I looked up at Abuela, who was watching me closely. *Just keep on moving, Martha,* I told myself. After lighting some sage and sweeping away the *mal,* I began the healing.

Abuela had shown me how to massage the stones into the body so that Señor Peña wouldn't have to pass them in pain. But it was difficult to do. I was still trying to find my *don.* According to Abuela, if I found it, I could use it to push healing power into the diseased area of the body. I tried focusing on breathing in and out evenly while I massaged in rhythm. I searched for the quiet place that I sometimes found during *reflexión.*

As I massaged, I didn't notice that Abuela had been walking around Señor Peña until I caught a flash of light from the corner of my eye. Instantly, my concentration broke, and I stopped massaging. Señor Peña, who had been lying down with his eyes closed, lifted his head and looked at me. I ignored him and turned to Abuela.

"What was that?" I asked.

She stood near Señor Peña's feet. "What was what?"

"That light."

Abuela's head cocked to the side and her eyes narrowed. "Nothing. Get back to healing."

I wanted to argue but instead let go a sigh of frustration. If my grandmother didn't want to tell me something, she wasn't going to tell me it, no matter how much I asked.

"Yes, finish please. I need to pick up *papas* for my wife for dinner," Señor Peña said.

"I am. I am."

I was about to close my eyes, because it helped me concentrate, when I suddenly noticed something near my hands. It was dark. I stopped and moved my hands away. Yes, it was right there, on Señor Peña's skin. Or, no, it wasn't *on* his skin. I reached out hesitantly and tried to brush away the dark spot, but it wouldn't go away.

I pulled my hand back. Señor Peña asked, "Is everything okay?"

I looked down and then back at him. Never make the patient uncomfortable. I tried my best to smile. "Yes, everything's fine." I began to massage again. He leaned back and closed his eyes.

But the spot didn't go away. I turned to search for Abuela but she had her back to me. She was doing something near the shelves that held the ingredients.

Moving my head closer, I tried to study the darkness further. It was beneath his skin, surrounding something. Oh, my God, this was crazy. I shook my head and closed my eyes. I was not seeing things. Nothing was there. I was dehydrated or tired or something. I worked on returning my breathing to an even state as I massaged. Breathe in for five counts and out five counts. I had just reached the point that it felt natural when . . . I felt it.

I've only had a panic attack once, and it sort of felt like that. My chest contracted and then as it spread open, it continued spreading and didn't stop. Of course, this is only how it felt. My chest didn't actually split open, but it felt like something was fighting to expand past my muscles and my chest cavity and my skin.

I didn't know if I was breathing and, in some ways, I couldn't even feel my body. I didn't know if I was still massaging Señor Peña or not. I couldn't stop it. I think I tried to fight it, but I'm not even sure if I can say that. Alarms were going off in my mind, and somehow I knew I could not fight it, that I had to give up.

And I did.

For anyone who has ever been on a river that was managed by a dam system, they know that the river barely runs when the gates to the dam are closed. One can relax on an inner tube in the same spot for hours . . . until the gate is opened. The water rises quickly over the next twenty minutes, spreading out into shallow channels with dirt embankments, until the water rises well beyond the peaks of the red muddy mounds, until they are no longer visible. The river runs swiftly, outward, filling each tendril of the small rivers and creeks that spread laterally from the main river.

That is what happened inside of me, or that is the best way I can describe it. Power flowed from my center and through my body, so that every cell in my being vibrated with power. I was the river when the gates of the dam were open, charged with new energy that intensified with every second.

I opened my eyes and saw that I was still massaging Señor Peña, but now there was something coming from my hands and it was going into the dark spot. It was light, but then it also wasn't light. That's about as well as I can describe it. I watched as the power consumed the darkness bit by bit until the darkness disappeared, all within a few minutes.

As soon as it was gone, I felt the light or power recede from my hands and from the other parts of my body, back toward the center of my chest. Although I couldn't see it, I felt it condense into a small pinpoint and move into some secret area inside of me, and immediately the gates closed.

I looked up and found Abuela standing at the end of the table, near Señor Peña's feet. "You felt it," she said.

I let go of a large breath and put my hands behind my head suddenly feeling dizzy. I didn't know how else to answer.

When Señor Peña left, with only a tiny bit more respect for me, I turned to Abuela, who had begun to wipe off the table that Señor Peña had been lying on with a rag and water.

"Good job, *m'ija*."

I sat down on the table, not caring that Abuela was still trying to wipe it down.

"Good job at what?" I said.

"You saw your *don*."

I stayed quiet for a few seconds. Abuela waited for me to respond. "I don't know if I did," I finally said.

She sat down next to me and put the rag in her lap. "You did. I saw it inside of you, saw you heal Señor Peña."

I heard what she said, but some part of me wasn't convinced. I had felt something, but it was stranger than anything I could imagine.

Abuela watched me. "I remember the first time I felt my *don*."

I turned and looked at her.

"My mother was helping a neighbor next door, and a young boy from the neighborhood came to the house, said his throat hurt. So I think, 'I can help him. I know some things.' But I was foolish. I didn't respect the gift I had."

"So what happened?" I asked.

"I placed my hands around his throat," she puts her hands out to demonstrate, "to see if his lymph nodes were swollen . . . and it happened. It only took a few minutes, but it was so much at once, that as soon as it was over, I screamed and ran to my room."

I started laughing. "You didn't!"

She smiled, "Don't tell anyone that story. Only Gloria knows of it because she found me huddled in the corner of my closet."

I laughed a bit more. "And the boy?"

"His throat was healed, but until this day, he is still scared of me." She smiled slyly.

Abuela placed her hand on mine. "It's a scary thing, *m'ija*. But it is also something amazing. You have the gift to help others, to truly make their lives better. Remember to respect it. Do not take it for granted, and do not use it unwisely."

I nodded and looked down. Abuela's hands were like my mother's: small, thin fingers with perfect, oval-shaped nails.

"So this means I'm a *curandera* now, huh?"

She stood up, "It isn't that easy, Martha." She threw the rag in a basket with other things that needed to be washed.

"What does that mean?"

"You asked about a light, before you felt your *don*. Do you know what that was?"

I thought about it. It wasn't from me. The light had come from near Abuela.

"Wait, were you healing Señor Peña? I thought I was healing his kidney stones?"

She said, "You were. While you were healing his kidney stones, I was keeping his arthritis from flaring."

"How were you healing him without touching him? And why didn't you just say you were healing when I asked?"

I stood up and walked over to her. She was starting to make a salve on the counter. She grabbed jars left and right, taking bits and pieces from each one.

"Those with our kind of gift do not need to touch someone to heal."

"Really?"

"*Sí.* You made a lot of progress today. You saw your *don* for the first time, and you healed your patient. But you can do a lot more with your gift."

More to learn? I had already memorized and made over two hundred different salves, potions, and mixtures. I had helped bring three babies into the world, massaged out arthritis and kidney stones and even set a few bones. Hell, I had even tried to cure *mal de ojo*, with

Abuela's guidance, and according to the patients, it had worked. Now she tells me I can heal from a distance? Always more to learn.

"So why didn't you just say what you were doing in front of Señor Peña?"

She started to grind the ingredients in a mortar with a pestle. "*Porque*, I didn't want him to know I was keeping his arthritis from flaring."

"But why? Shouldn't he know?"

She stopped grinding, put the pestle down and turned to me. "We are *curanderas*. If they knew we healed without touching them, what would they say? *¡Brujas!* We aren't witches . . . we just have gifts they cannot understand."

"And the cures we give them? The massages? Do they even matter if we can heal them without touching them?"

"Of course. Material cures are from the earth, as are we. Our spiritual gifts are extras in healing. Why use our spiritual gifts if we can just make them a tea? Better on them, better for us."

I asked what she meant by that, "better for us."

She told me that using too much of one's *don* could wear out a *curandera*, even make her pass out. And in extreme cases, perhaps die.

It was a Saturday when Abuela sent me to the market area downtown. Doña Lorena was going to fit me for my Christmas dress, which I feared would be a red and green, velvety disaster. The fitting didn't take long, and before I left, Doña Lorena gave me a bag with a new nightgown for Abuela. I left and decided to find Sofía's Cosas, the boutique Laura's mother ran. I almost walked past it, since the sign was only about eight by eight inches and hung on a nail next to the door.

I looked around to make sure no one watched me before I went in. Wouldn't do for someone to go tattle to Abuela that I was at a business run by Laura's mom, a woman she despised . . . for a reason I still didn't know.

I stepped in and began to look around. The store was full of knickknacks, hanging on the walls, stacked on tables, piled on the floor. There was a large collection of pottery plates, hand-painted with Aztec-like symbols hanging on the wall next to an assortment of crosses ranging from large to small, wooden to metal. Some things were still wrapped in their plastic bags, while clothing and scarves were set on display cases, scrunched close together to allow more room for other knickknacks and baubles. There was a large section of candles of all different colors and sizes. Some had the Virgin Mary's picture glued on the front and some had Santa Muerte's picture, the Saint of Death, who helped keep the balance in the world. The shop did not lack in piñatas, kites, peasant skirts or huaraches, either. The store smelled of must and dust, and if there had been more lighting, I am sure I would have seen tiny dust particles floating among the mass of things.

After a moment, I noticed that I was the only person in the store.

"You're here!" someone whispered.

I stepped to the right and saw Laura's head peeking between a mass of jewelry stands on the checkout counter. She disappeared for a second as she ran around the counter to meet me.

"Come on," she said grabbing my arm and pulling me to the counter.

"Laura, I don't have a lot of time."

"And you think I do? My mom would kill me if she knew you were here. She doesn't want to piss your *abuela* off."

Behind the counter she let go of my arm. I placed the bag Doña Lorena had given me next to some jewelry stands.

Laura bent down to one of the bottom shelves pushed up against the wall. They were full of binders and folders with papers sticking out of them. From between a blue spiral and a Lisa Frank unicorn folder, she pulled out a stack of postcards and one envelope.

"What's all this?" I asked.

"This is what I wanted to show you."

She handed me the first postcard.

"Made it to Dallas," I read. "I'll send you another one soon." Beneath the words was some kind of drawing. A flower maybe? "What's that? I don't get it."

"That little drawing on every postcard . . . it's a signature. It took me awhile to figure it out. Look at this letter."

I grabbed the letter and opened it. Inside was a picture, a Polaroid. I turned it over . . . a baby wrapped in a blanket. Eyes shut tight, hands curled in fists and bottom lip pouting.

"Is that you?" I asked.

Laura shook her head no.

I opened the letter.

She's beautiful, isn't she? That's what everyone says. All I see is my own stupidity and another face that I will never know.

Living in Raleigh for a bit. Maybe we will move up the coast when I get back to work and make a little bit of money. How is she? You helped me so much . . . and then this happens.

Will you give Juanita the letter I included with this? She's got a million hiding spaces at home. No worries about my mother finding it.

Miss you. Rosa.

It was a rose. The drawing was a rose.

It was quiet for a second, and then Laura spoke. "The last one was sent in 1973."

My birth year. They were postcards from my mother, and that Polaroid was a picture of me. I turned it over. A tiny baby. I didn't even recognize myself.

"I looked through all the postcards. They're from your mom, right?" Laura said.

"Yeah . . . her handwriting's changed a lot . . ." I turned and looked at Laura. "So your mom and my mom were close?"

Laura nodded. "I figured they kind of were, being cousins and all . . . but these prove they were *really* close. Think they were the same age. She never talks about your mom, but I found these the other day between those folders. I don't know why my mom would hide them."

I held up one of the postcards. It was a postcard from Monroe, Louisiana, featuring a bayou. Did Laura's mom and my mother's friendship have something to do with why Abuela and Laura's mom had a falling out?

"You thinking what I'm thinking?" Laura asked.

"I think this is . . . weird. I really don't know . . . " Suddenly, someone from the back shouted Laura's name.

"Damn it!" Laura whispered. She grabbed the post-card and the one letter and shoved them between the folders. "It's my mom. Darn! She never comes out on Saturday."

A door opened in the back. Laura pushed me from behind the counter and to the door, but as we were running, I remembered the bag that I had left on the counter. I turned around and ran back for it. As soon as my hand latched onto the bag, a woman came into view.

"Hello, welcome to . . . " Her words trailed off.

We stood there, Laura's mom and me, looking at each other. Her jaw moved as if she wanted to say something but didn't know what. She had a mass of dark, tiny curls that circled her face and stopped at her shoulders, which was weird because Laura's hair was so straight. The loose, black dress she wore hung on her thin frame, and her wrists were covered with large, wooden bangles that I had seen on one of the jewelry stands on the check-out counter. She looked older than my mother . . . maybe it was because she had on no make-up, not even lipstick.

Finally she spoke. "Laura, go make some coffee."

I felt Laura walk up next to me. "Mom . . . I, she was just leaving. She needed . . . "

"Laura." Her mom crossed her arms slowly over her chest. "Go."

Laura didn't look at me as she walked past her mom and disappeared to the back. Laura's mom walked toward me.

"You must be Martha."

"Um, yes, I . . . "

"I'm Sofía." She held out her hand to me.

Hesitantly, I shook it. She gave me a small smile, then walked around the counter and stood behind it.

"So did you come by my store to shop?"

"Yeah, um, Laura told me about it. Thought I'd look for a birthday gift . . . for a friend. But I think I should go now."

"What friend? What do they like?" She leaned forward onto her elbows.

"I should go, if Abuela knew I was here . . . "

Sofía pushed off the counter and threw her hands above her in a mocking manner. "The heavens would pour down with María's wrath."

Her face was serious for a moment, but then she smiled. I couldn't help it and smiled too. She was funny. Why didn't Abuela like Sofía?

"Don't worry, Martha, I won't let this get back to her. Just because she's mad at me doesn't mean she should take it out on you. Or my daughter."

I walked forward a little. "What is she mad at exactly? No one will say."

Sofía picked up some necklaces that had fallen off their stand and hung them back up. "Martha, you will find out that this family keeps secrets about everything. They think if we keep it quiet, it never happened. It will all go away."

"I've noticed," I said.

Sofía paused in her movements, then hung the last necklace. "Look, I know your grandmother wouldn't want this known, but the reason she and I . . . don't speak . . . is because I helped your mother out a long time ago."

"That's it? Abuela's mad because you helped my mother?"

Sofía crossed her arms beneath her chest. "I helped her out with something pretty big, and your grandmother didn't like that . . . at all."

"Helped her out with what?"

Sofía smiled. "It's not the 'what' that really matters. And it's not really important anymore. The main thing is that your grandmother can hold a grudge."

"Thought you said secrets were bad."

"No, I said this family keeps secrets to pretend like things never happened."

"So you're going to keep this a secret from me?"

"I'm sure you'll find out one day. But for now, you need to get home without your grandmother finding out you've been here."

"But . . . "

"Martha," her voice took on the authoritative tone she had used with Laura earlier. She was almost as scary as Abuela in that moment.

Sofía let me go out the back door so that no one would see me leave. When I got home I found a wooden bracelet, just like the one Sofía was wearing, in the bag Doña Lorena had given me. Did Sofía sneak it in? I snatched it out before Abuela could see it and kept it hidden in my backpack until I had the chance to leave it in my locker at school.

Laura and I didn't talk about that Saturday at lunch on Monday. Guess we figured if we kept quiet, it never actually happened.

After reading my mother's letter and finding out she'd sent Tía Juanita one as well, I couldn't stop wondering if Juanita had hidden it and if it was still in the house. The next day, I was looking for the letter when

Abuela asked me to change the sheets on my bed. In my unorganized attempt to take off everything at once, so I could hurry back to searching, I kicked a pillowcase beneath the bed. I dropped to my belly to grab it, and as soon as I pulled it out, I noticed something hidden between the wooden slats of the bed frame.

I don't know how it caught my eye. It would have been easy to miss because only a small, purple corner was visible in the center of the bed frame. I pushed myself forward with my elbows until I was able to reach up and slide it through the slats. When I finally pulled it free, I saw it was a purple, leather journal.

I scooted out from beneath the bed and sat up with my back against the frame. It wasn't a letter, but maybe it was something better? What if this was my mother's? I had searched this room last night, even searched the bathroom and living room, but I hadn't found a single thing. I did, however, find a few places that I thought had been old hiding spots because they were pretty crafty but they were all empty. One was a hollow leg that screwed off a stool in the closet! Either Juanita had emptied them or I had just missed good hiding spots, spots that would never be found.

But I had never thought to look in the slats of the bed frame. It couldn't be this easy, could it? Maybe I wouldn't even have to find Carlita or the letter.

I opened the journal and found nothing on the first page. Disappointed, I turned a few more pages until I found handwriting. To my disappointment, it wasn't my mother's handwriting. I flipped to the front cover to see if there was a name, but it wasn't until I flipped to the back cover that I found blue cursive handwriting: Juanita Gonzalez.

I closed the book. What should I do? Give it to Juanita or read it? It might have some clues to why my mother disappeared or the secrets everyone kept from me. Or maybe it could at least tell me about the letter? I opened the journal again: no dates. I needed the journal to be around 1971, 1972 or 1973, my mother's last two years in high school and the year I was born. Without dates, this journal might start and end way before or way after my mother had left. I grunted in annoyance.

I didn't have time to think, though, because Abuela yelled for me from the kitchen, where she was hand-washing her sheets, ready for mine. I stuffed the journal beneath the mattress, quickly got up and grabbed the sheets.

On Monday I took the journal to school because I didn't want Abuela to know I had it. I would never have time to read it at her house, anyway. I read the journal before class began, in study hall and every free moment I had. I kept it in my backpack and, before I left school, locked it in my locker.

Juanita's handwriting had exaggerated loops and curves, so at first it was difficult to read the entries. At least it was in English. After a few tries, I was able to decipher the first page.

Sister Bertha gave me this journal. She asked to see me after Sunday school one day and handed me this beautiful book. I didn't even know nuns had money to buy things! Anyways, she asked me to write down my thoughts every day and to bring it to her at the end of every month. She said it was important to use full sentences and to write down every detail. I asked her why she wanted me to keep a journal. I never have before!

*She said she noticed I had difficulty expressing myself,
not just in Sunday school class, but with Mamá and
Rosa too. Can you believe it? I mean, I never thought
about it, but I guess she's right. They are just so loud
and strong and sometimes they don't listen to me. Sister
Bertha says this will help. And even if it doesn't, what
can it hurt? Besides, I can't say no to a nun!*

After the first page, I read three pages of Juanita
explaining her life, as if she had to introduce herself to
the journal. After that she began to write about her days
in so much detail that I wanted to poke my eyes out!
Who cared about what she ate and every single step she
took that day? Did she really need to write down that she
went to the bathroom after lunch?

Then I came to the *quinceañera* section. Juanita was
almost fifteen and obsessed with *quinceañeras*. She
planned every single detail out in her journal: the location, her court, the crown, the shoes . . . she even drew
a crude drawing of what she wanted her dress to look
like. Apparently nothing went the way she wanted,
because there were five pages of rants about how her
mother got everything wrong, her dress was ugly and
the decorations weren't as cool as some girl named
Roselia's, and to top it all off Juanita's uncle got drunk
and embarrassed her with a slurred speech in front of
everyone in which he continually repeated, "*M'ija*, we
love you!"

Finally, I came to a passage about my mother. Juanita mentioned that Abuela would begin teaching my
mother *curanderismo*. I punched the air in relief and
excitement when I read that sentence. Thank God! This
had to be around 1971. No more stupid dresses or talks

about boys and friends! Juanita was a little jealous of this, but she was hopeful that maybe one day her mother would see the gift in her too. My mother was learning how to be a *curandera* . . . something I was doing now.

Funny: I had never thought about it before, but my mother and I had never had anything in common, except the gift.

Ocho

FOR THE NEXT FEW DAYS I couldn't put the journal down. Although most of the entries were useless: Juanita writing about her day, someone she liked, who she had kissed. I was too scared to skip over anything. I didn't want to miss something significant.

I almost fell out of my chair at lunch one day when I read a very small passage about my mother winning homecoming queen. Juanita didn't seem too happy when she wrote, *Rosa won't shut up about her stupid dress and stupid crown.* I was elated. The journal entry was from around 1972, the year that my mother's life changed.

Each time my mother or Abuela's name popped up, I would stop and go over the entry, trying to read between the lines, trying to see something that wasn't there. It wasn't until I had read over half of the journal that something interesting finally came up. I was in math class and had already finished my worksheet, so I was free to do whatever I wanted, like read.

Rosa has been a puta lately. She keeps sneaking out the house at night to meet up with Jorge and then she expects me to lie for her! She doesn't even say thanks! She's moody all day and pissed off. Mamá and her are

*fighting so loud that I can't concentrate on writing this!
They shout about nothing most of the time!*

Was this it? I read the next page.

*Rosa is refusing to help Mamá with her healing. She
says she's too busy but I know she is lying and it has
something to do with Jorge. I can hear Rosa and Jorge
arguing through the window when she's sneaking back
at night. I think Jorge wants to get married or something stupid like that. It's hard to hear. Doesn't Rosa
know how lucky she is? She's such an idiot.*

The bell interrupted my reading, forcing me to go to
the cafeteria for lunch. I packed up my binder and note-
book but kept the journal out. I was planning on reading
it as soon as I sat down. I got in line, grabbed a tray, a
burger and fries. A line had formed at the cashier. I
looked ahead. Some guy was arguing with the lady about
something while he searched through his backpack.
Probably lost his money.

I grabbed a fry from my tray and popped it into my
mouth. Might as well read a page while I waited.

*I could kill Rosa! We had the biggest fight today. I
walked into the bathroom and she was just standing
over the sink, one hand on her head, and she was
breathing frantically like she was having a breakdown
or something. Her face was pale and I thought she was
going to throw up or faint or something. When I asked
if she was okay, she went crazy on me! She started
yelling at me to get out, to mind my own damn business. That's what I get for being such a good sister? My*

own sister calling me a puta? Damn her. I hope Mamá
finds out.

The next instant, the journal was out of my hand flying in an arc away from me. It took me a second to realize
that Marcela had walked past me with her friends, laughing. She had grabbed the journal and had thrown it on the
floor before pouring a full carton of milk all over it.

"Hey!" I dropped my tray and a loud clang echoed
throughout the cafeteria. I pushed past Marcela, hitting
her shoulder with mine as I did. She stumbled back and
I glimpsed her pissed-off face.

"Fuck!" I didn't care who heard. I squatted down slowly and picked up the journal, careful not to get milk on
me. It was hopeless. Half the journal was soaked through,
the blue ink bleeding into misshapen blobs. I shook off
some of the milk and looked through the dry pages. Most
of them were at the beginning of the journal—stuff I'd
already read! The dry pages at the back of the journal
were starting to get moist and stick to the wet pages.
Damn it. I had been getting somewhere. I felt it, I was
about to find out. And even if I wasn't, I would never
know now. Marcela had taken that from me.

My neck grew warm, and then warmer, and then
burning hot. Anger built up in me. Sweat formed on my
brow. I dropped the journal back into the milk. It was
useless, gone, done. My only chance was gone, and
Marcela was to blame. She had caused this.

I turned around and spit out, "You bitch!"

I moved toward Marcela, ready to push her, slap her,
when a man called out, "Hey, you! Put that down, now!"

Marcela held a knife in her hand and was walking
toward me. We both stopped as soon as she heard the

voice. The cafeteria was quiet. Everyone watched us. The man, a young teacher on duty, walked up swiftly. I lowered my fist.

Marcela still held the knife. She looked at me, her eyes black and her shoulders tensed. What was she going to do with that knife? Stab me? I felt her anger across the short distance. It pulsed, over and over again. At least, I thought it was anger until, suddenly, something happened with my vision and I saw that it wasn't anger that was pulsing out of Marcela. It was something more—she had a *don*? It looked just like Abuela's *don* but different. Marcela's was darker, warped.

No, that couldn't be it. No . . . I shook my head a little and my vision cleared so that all that stood in front of me was Marcela.

"I said, *put it down*." The man now stood on Marcela's left, about a foot or two away.

Her hand tightened on the knife for one second before she dropped it. One, two, three, four, five tiny pings echoed through the large silent room, until the knife lay flat on the floor.

"Principal. Now!" The man grabbed Marcela's elbow and dragged her away.

Marcela and I had reached a new level of hate for each other.

After the teacher took Marcela to the principal's office, I walked out. No one spoke to me, no teacher stopped and asked if I was okay. I did hear a guy say, "Why didn't Martha just zap her with her witch power?" There were a few snickers from the surrounding tables, but when I looked at them, they stopped quickly and tried looking anywhere but at me.

I left the journal where it was. Somebody else could throw it away. It was no use to me now. I felt bad that I couldn't give it back to Juanita, but she had forgotten it anyway and wouldn't miss it now.

When I got to the hallway, I thought I heard someone call my name. Maybe it was Laura. I didn't stop, and no one came after me.

I couldn't quite say how the rest of my classes went. My body went through the motions, but I wasn't there. I was thinking too hard about Marcela. I had felt it in the cafeteria: her power. Didn't I? It was all in her anger. And Laura had been right: Marcela really *did* have the gift, or some kind of gift, since she hadn't exactly been trying to heal me.

But that was crazy. It couldn't have been a *don*. Could *dons* look like that? They were gifts meant for healing. What did you call a gift not meant for healing? Could you use it for evil? And why did I see it? Or did I? This was becoming too much. All this *curandera-bruja* crap. Because that's what it was. Crap. I didn't sign up for this. Seeing things that weren't even there.

And if Marcela did have a *don* . . . and I'm not saying she did . . . but if she did, Abuela would have seen it in Marcela the day she came to the house asking to be her apprentice. And she turned Marcela away. Why? If there hadn't been anyone else that had come along with the gift, and if Marcela did have one, then why not accept her as an apprentice? Perhaps the difference between Marcela and me was that she had picked up a knife and I hadn't. Is that what Abuela had seen in her? That capability?

And what did that say about me? That I was a safe bet, or was it only because I was her granddaughter?

By the end of the day, there were a lot of rumors about Marcela and me. A lot of people had heard that Marcela really had stabbed me. In my physics class, one girl turned to her friend and said, "See? I told you, nothing happened to her." I wanted to punch this one guy during last period when he tapped my shoulder and said, "Is it true you stopped her with your mind?" I rolled my eyes and replied, "Don't be stupid." He just shrugged and turned back to the teacher.

There was one rumor that was true. Marcela was expelled for pulling a knife and sent to a juvenile detention center for two weeks, which meant I wouldn't have to see her until next semester, since school would be out in exactly two weeks for winter break. I got detention for two days. Thank you, Mr. Principal. At least, I wouldn't have to watch my back for awhile . . . in school at least.

At the end of the day, Abuela waited for me outside my last class. My detention would begin next week.

"Why are you here?"

The corners of her lips fell farther down her face, stretching out the skin of her flabby cheeks. She didn't say anything but turned and began walking to the front of the school. Abuela's forceful steps were a billboard for her anger. Someone had told Abuela about the incident with Marcela. Still, I hadn't imagined she would pick me up.

Abuela had brought the gold Cadillac and parked it on the left side of the school, right in the way of everyone else who was trying to pick up their kids. Either Abuela didn't care or she didn't realize what she had done. It was probably a combination of the two. We got into the car, and Abuela took off, jumping into the traffic seamlessly as if the traffic had been waiting for her to pull out.

Her hands gripped the steering wheel so tightly her knuckles were white. She looked straight ahead, leaning forward in her seat, so that her large chest almost touched the steering wheel. Her lips were pursed, as they always were when she was angry.

Once we made it into the neighborhood, only a few minutes away from the school, Abuela spoke, "What did I tell you? I said stay away from that girl!"

I had been slouched before, but feeling attacked, I sat up in my seat. "I *did* stay away! And she started it!"

"So, you think it's okay to retaliate? To push her? To raise your fist? Over a book?" How the hell did she know all this?

"You weren't even there. You don't know the whole story. She . . . "

"*Ay*, she is nothing! You! I said, stay away from her and you don't listen. How can I trust you?!"

I yelled back. "Trust me? How can I trust you? You changed my freaking last name! Who does that?"

"I can do whatever I please! You are a Gonzalez whether you like . . . "

"You never tell me anything! I've done all you've asked, and you blame me for stuff . . . "

Abuela's voice rose louder. "Of course, I blame you. I expect more from you, and you let me down, just like your mother!"

She slammed on the brakes, and I was jerked forward in my seat belt. For a moment I couldn't breathe because the seat cut into my chest then all at once I was slammed back into the seat.

I shouted when I could breathe again, "God!"

I turned to Abuela, fuming and wishing she was Marcela so I could hit her. The area just below Abuela's white hairline was tinged in pink, and her eyes were dark with a similar rage I had witnessed earlier.

"Go. I need to do some things," she said through gritted teeth.

I turned and looked out of the window. We were at Juanita's house.

I jerked my seat belt off and pushed the door open, but before I stepped out, I turned back. "I'm not my mother. But it's not hard to see why she left this place. She couldn't stand your craziness!"

I hopped out of the car and slammed the door. Stomping to the house, I silently cussed Abuela out with every single bad word I could think of in Spanish and in English.

My grandmother sped off with a screech of her tires. I was once again reminded of the day my mother left me.

Nueve

JUANITA GAVE ME MY SPACE, at least for a little bit. I flew past her when she opened the door, stomped through the hallway into the kitchen and then out the back door. I dropped my backpack on the ground before I threw myself into an old, woven green lawn chair. I was left alone for about an hour, seething in anger.

How could Abuela think that I was anything like my mother? She was delusional. I couldn't stand her crazy mood swings and the ridiculous stuff that came out of her mouth. No wonder my mother had left. There's your answer, Martha! She left because her mother was a lunatic.

Juanita came outside with two *panes de dulce* and a glass of milk. She sat down in the other lawn chair next to me. She placed the glass of milk and the sweet bread on a small, plastic table between us. It was warm outside but not necessarily hot, since it was the beginning of December. Or perhaps I had grown used to the heat, as I had grown so used to other things: the brown people, the language, the food, the life. I just hadn't recognized my comfort with it until now.

I refused to look at Juanita. Looking at her would remind me of the journal, and the journal would remind me of the fact that I wasn't any closer to finding out why my mother had left or where she was. I wanted so badly to ask Juanita what she had known, why my mother had left. But she wouldn't tell me, and even if she did tell me, she'd run and tell Abuela, and then Abuela would do everything to keep me from searching.

"When your mother and I were little, we used to run away sometimes."

Oh, so my mother learned to run away early. That would have been a nice warning.

She continued, "She would wake me up in the middle of the night with a bag full of clothes and snacks and tell me to be quiet as we snuck out of the house. But we never got farther than down the street before we got too scared and would run to the backyard, pretending we were somewhere we weren't."

"Why did you want to run away?"

"C'mon, Martha. You can't imagine why? "

"Let me guess, the big bad I-want-to-control-every-thing wolf?"

"Of course." She grabbed a *pan de dulce*, tore a piece off and threw it in her mouth. I took the other one and did the same, except I dipped my piece into the glass of milk before eating the sugary deliciousness.

"Why is she like that? It's so hard to live with some-one like her."

Juanita chuckled. "You think it was easy for me and Rosa? You have it much easier, trust me."

"I doubt it. She expects so much from me! *Curandera* work. Good grades. Stay out of trouble. I didn't ask for all of this. When I came here, all I wanted . . . "

"Wanted what?"

Was to be invisible. But I couldn't say that. "Nothing. It's just so much."

Juanita put her hand on my shoulder. "Martha, do you want to be a *curandera*? Do you even like learning those things?"

I shrugged. "Yeah, I mean I did. I do. I don't know right now. It's a lot of work, and sometimes I don't even know if I'm doing it right or doing anything at all . . . if it's even real."

She nodded her head. "I understand. But look, you don't have to do it if you don't want to. You can be a normal kid. I can ask Mamá to stop teaching you. Whatever you want."

Is that what I wanted? Although I wish I could say it was, it wasn't. I did like learning this stuff. Even if healing from a distance or seeing someone's *don* seemed impossible, I knew the physical cures worked. I had seen it myself. The teas, the pastes, the massages, they were the real deal. And I enjoyed that. If I didn't have *curandera* work, what would I have? Who would I be without it? Who would I become?

"No, don't do that. Maybe just get Abuela off my back a little."

Juanita took another bite. "Look Martha, your *abuela,* she doesn't understand some things. She was brought up in a different time with different ideals. And she's a stubborn, strong woman. She won't ever admit that she's wrong."

"Well, she should! She can't use her upbringing as an excuse. I don't."

"Don't you?"

I started to flick my wrist at Juanita but caught myself. I stared at my hand in horror. Oh, shit . . . no, that didn't mean anything! I was nothing like Abuela. *Nothing* like her.

Juanita waited, so I quickly said, "Whatever."

We sat there and let a few moments pass by, finishing our sweet bread.

"Martha, I really am proud of you. I know no one has said it, but you've carried yourself well, especially with everything that's happened. Your mother and all. I just want you to know that people do notice."

I didn't respond, just sat there trying not to let the lump in my throat rise up and spill over.

Instead, I asked, "So why did you and my mom run away? The first time, I mean."

Juanita screwed her face up in thought. "You know, I don't even remember." She laughed. "We tend to forget those things that we found so important at the time they happened."

I looked at Juanita. She was different from the girl of the journal. She wasn't hyper-excited, pitying herself or obsessive about material things any longer. Actually, Juanita wasn't too bad.

Something else bothered me. "Will you be honest with me?"

She nodded yes.

"Do you know where my mother is?"

She leaned back in her seat and looked across the front yard. "Martha, I wish I did."

"If you did know where she was, would you tell me?"

She opened her mouth, then closed it quickly. She brushed a strand of hair from her forehead and shook her head no. "I don't think I would."

"Why?"

"Martha, you have to understand that Rosa was never good at . . . relationships. Not even with me. Once, she got so pissed at me for not agreeing with her that she left me in Mexico, so I had to find my way home, alone. I was only twelve."

"But, that doesn't mean . . . "

Juanita interrupted me. "She wanted to leave, Martha," she paused. "And sometimes we are better off if some things are never found. Even if those things are people."

Abuela and I didn't speak that night when she picked me up from Juanita's. We didn't speak on the car ride home, nor did we speak when Gloria greeted us in the kitchen with dinner. We didn't even speak during the meal. When Gloria finally figured out that no one would converse with her, she got up, stomped to the cupboard and pulled the mini television out, switched it to a *telenovela* and ignored us.

I didn't find out where Abuela had gone during the day. It didn't concern me much at all, until I woke up the next morning and found that Abuela had burned three candles for protection throughout the night and had left an amulet beside the candles. I stared at the flickering flames, then picked up the amulet. It surprised me that the candles had not melted during the night, just like those candles from my first night at Abuela's.

The amulet, a leather pouch, smelled strongly of garlic, which was confirmed by the clove I found inside. There were also a few gold coins, a red ribbon and a piece of lodestone. Wherever Abuela went yesterday, whatever she encountered, made her believe that I was in serious trouble, because the amulet was the strongest protection that Abuela knew. Still, what could this little sack do against Marcela? I hated to admit it, but my faith was shaken when it came to some of the *curandera* stuff. I just didn't know what to believe.

The next day was Saturday. Abuela still wasn't speaking to me, but we had patients to take care of at their houses. Even though I still was an apprentice to Abuela, I was pretty skilled in a lot of things by this time and a bit more independent. Or at least, I thought I was. I had also been practicing healing without touching patients. It took a lot of concentration, but I could do it. At least I thought I could. Sometimes I just wasn't sure if what I was doing was real, if what I was feeling wasn't some ludicrous self-fulfilling prophecy bullshit that I had created, thanks to a little push from Abuela.

But then when I healed . . . I felt my *don* and was sort of convinced that it was real. That build-up of power at the center of my chest . . . a ball of energy pushing outward into what felt like an empty cavity: it pushed with so much force that I thought I might throw up . . . and then, suddenly, I would breathe and the energy would spread out and everything inside me vibrated with *something*. Something would make my head woozy and my body loose . . . . From there, my *don* found the sickness in the patient, and I healed the sickness away. I mean, one moment it was there, all dark and blotchy like a blind spot in my vision, and the next it was gone. And when I was done, my *don* returned to the center of my chest, almost cutting off my breath until as quickly as it came, it disappeared and I was left wondering if it had ever happened at all.

As we were leaving the house, Abuela said, "Here," and shoved a paper bag at me. "Go to Juan Pedrito's and give him the *alcanfor* for his rheumatism. Then go see Señora Gallos and give her the herbs. I'll meet you at

Doña Cristelia's." She turned and walked down the street in the opposite direction, leaving me with the bag and nothing else.

That was it? Looked like I would mostly be administering physical cures. And not really even that. This lady was killing me.

Juan Pedrito was an old widower whose rheumatism was so bad that his left hand had curled into a claw. When I arrived at his house, I went inside and made him a tea with the herbs Abuela had placed in the bag for him. Then I massaged both his right hand and his left hand claw with the camphor oil Abuela had placed in a little bottle. It stung the skin of my palms a bit, but it was nothing I couldn't handle. Thirty minutes later I was finished, he thanked me and I left.

Señora Gallos' house was a different story. She needed more herbs to prevent pregnancy. She had seven children already, and her husband couldn't keep his hands off her. They could barely afford the ones they already had. Most of the children I had seen on the visits to the Gallos house ran around without shoes, and their clothes were either too big or too tight on their skinny bodies.

When I arrived at the house, she greeted me, *"Buenas,* Martha, *ven,* come in, quickly now."

Although everyone in her neighborhood had come to see Abuela many times, Señora Gallos was nervous that if anyone saw her with the *curanderas,* they'd gossip about her, just as she gossiped about them. Sometimes I didn't understand the people of Laredo. They respected the *curandera* and *curandero* but whispered lies or rumors of witchcraft. They begged the *curandera* for cures but then denied their association with them. God forbid anyone just admit the truth in this town!

Then again the people that had opened *yerberías*, herb shops, around the neighborhoods weren't helping the *curandera* name, either. They promised healings for a small price and many people with hope had flocked to the stores for convenience or in desperation, only to have their money stolen and be left with no cure. Because of those frauds there were a lot of people who didn't believe that *curanderas* had gifts and who thought that we were only out to make money off sick people and their hopes and sufferings.

Abuela was one of the last few honest *curanderas* in Laredo. It was fake *curanderas* and Señora Gallos' fear that were making things difficult for Abuela and annoying as hell for me.

After I stepped into her living room, I gave Señora Gallos the bag with the remaining herbs to make the birth control tea.

"*Muchas gracias*, these save my life." She held on tightly to the bag and closed her eyes for a moment. She looked relieved. "Men. Stay away from them . . . they just want to give you children and then no money to feed them, *verdad*?"

I nodded and said, "*Verdad*," as if I really knew what she meant.

"I have a bag of plantains for your *abuela*, fresh from Mexico. I'll go get them."

I told her thank you, but Abuela would decline if she were here.

"Nonsense!" she said. "I insist!"

When patients offered to give Abuela something in payment, Abuela always refused and had told me to do the same. However, it was rude to not accept the gift if the patient insisted—a cultural thing I had only learned when I continually said "no" to a customer one day and was berated by Abuela after the patient left the house. She told me Mexicans are proud, and we must not hurt their pride by refusing their gifts.

Couldn't they just be like normal people? Then maybe we wouldn't have to go through the traditional "No, thank you—I insist" two step. However, I couldn't complain too much. I think it was how we got most of our groceries.

As I stood waiting, I felt a tap on my shoulder. I turned, almost called out, because I wasn't expecting someone to approach me from behind. I caught myself when I saw the girl's expression in front of me. It was Señora Gallos' oldest daughter, Leta. She was a freshman at my school, but I had never spoken to her.

"I have to ask you something before my mother returns," she whispered, her eyes darting to the doorway where her mother had disappeared. "I moved the plantains, so it'll take her a few minutes to find them. Can I ask you a question?"

"Yeah, what is it?"

Leta looked on the verge of crying.

"Are you okay?"

Her hands nervously jumped around her. Pushing her hair back. Grabbing her arm. Cracking her knuckles. "You're not a *bruja*, are you? Everyone whispers. Do you know anything, really? I don't know if I should talk to you."

"No, I'm learning to be a *curandera*. Not a *bruja*. Totally different. Do you need something or not?" I could have been nicer, but I was only sixteen, and little things like this annoyed me.

Leta nodded but didn't appear to want to say. "If I tell, you have to keep it a secret, yes? Not tell anyone? That is your job? Not even to your *abuela,* right?"

It was the first time someone had asked me to keep a secret as a *curandera*. "Yes," I said, fearing Señora Gallos would return before I was given this chance to keep my own *curandera*-patient secret. I momentarily forgot my loss of faith in *curanderismo* and was once again excited.

"Okay, I haven't, you know," Leta paused, cringing, then said, "had my period in two months, and sometimes I get dizzy and I'm always hungry. And the last few days, I've been throwing up every morning. Am I . . . ," she leaned forward and whispered, "pregnant?"

I first thought, yeah, of course, if those are your symptoms, then you're probably pregnant, but I would need to check to make sure. I was about to give her my answer, when something else occurred to me. Journal: . . . *thought she was going to throw up or faint . . . moody all day . . . Rosa and Jorge arguing. I hope Mamá finds out?*

No . . . it couldn't . . . but it made sense . . . I mean . . . holy shit! It was there in the diary. . . . It had been in the words of the diary. Holy hell . . .

"Martha? Hurry, am I or am I not?"

I swallowed, feeling a small amount of spit coat my throat as it made its way down. "I . . . uh . . . yeah, I think so. But I would have to check to make sure." I couldn't breathe. This wasn't happening. My thoughts shifted back and forth from the present reality to a disturbing realization.

Leta was on the verge of crying. "I'll let you know." She ran off through a different doorway, taking fast, deep gulps of air. As soon as she disappeared, her mother walked into the room.

"I found them! I thought I had put them in the pantry, but they were under the table. I . . . " She stopped when she saw the strange look on my face. "Martha? ¿*Todo bien*?"

I wanted to shake my head no. No, everything was *not* okay. But I didn't do that. I nodded and then said, "Yes, I'm fine. Thank you, but I need to go."

I turned and walked out the front door and didn't stop, even when Señora Gallos yelled, "Wait, the plantains! You forgot them!"

I didn't care about the plantains. I walked and walked, not sure where I was going to.

Diez

I walked past Doña Cristelia's house. I didn't know if Abuela was in there or not, but I couldn't look at her yet. I couldn't look at anyone. My tennis shoes slapped hard against the concrete as I walked by colored house after tacky-colored house after tackier-colored house. The noise of my shoes was the only thing I could focus on, had to focus on. I kept walking faster and faster, until finally I started to jog and then run at a full sprint. I kept running and running until I finally saw the pink house. I ran up the stairs onto the porch and stopped. My breath was coming hard as I stood panting for air, my shirt sticking to my back and chest.

I turned around and hit the house with the side of my fist. When I pulled my hand back a few pieces of pink paint flakes had come off. I wiped my hand on my shorts and sat down on the porch with my knees bent and my forearms crossed over the tops of them.

My fists were clenched and shaking. *I* was shaking.

My mother had been pregnant. That was it. That was the secret all along. It made perfect sense. She had been hiding her pregnancy from Abuela.

Even worse, though, was that she hadn't been pregnant with me. The journal hadn't had dates or anything, but it had been clear that this was my mother's senior

171

year. Unless my mother had been pregnant for almost two years, then it couldn't have been me. I wouldn't have been born until about a year and a half later, maybe two years later.

Did she have the baby? Did Abuela find out, or did my mother get rid of the baby with an herbal remedy or her own hands? If she had the baby, where was it? Somehow I had a feeling that Abuela had found out about it. That had to be why my mother left. And Jorge had to be the father. He had known! That's why he had refused to speak to me. That had to be it. And he didn't even tell me. Or did my mother keep the baby a secret from him and he was just mad at her for leaving him?

Oh, God. I had a freaking brother or sister. How the hell was this kept from me?

I put my head into my hands.

"Martha!"

I looked up. Abuela was wobbling toward the house and she didn't look too happy.

"Why didn't you meet me at Doña Cristelia's? What happened? Are you okay?"

I pushed myself up so that I was standing when Abuela reached the porch. I opened my mouth to respond but closed it when I couldn't think of something to say.

My hands were still shaking.

She finally made it to the top step and looked me over. "What's wrong with you? *¿Qué pasó?* What happened?"

Her eyes searched my face for an answer. What had she done when she had found out?

"I . . . I just didn't feel good," I finally responded.

She squinted and I knew she was looking me over with her *don*, but she wouldn't find anything. Had she done the same thing to my mother? Looked her over one day with her *don* and realized? How long had it taken until Abuela could see the truth?

"Get inside." She walked inside the house, holding the door open for me. All of a sudden, I *did* feel sick. Sick at the thought of what I had discovered. Sick at the thought of what I would find, because I couldn't just stop now. I had to know what happened to the baby and to my mother.

After entering the house, I walked straight to my room and lay down on my bed. I heard her in her work-room, rummaging through things. Minutes later, she was in the kitchen throwing things around. A little later, when I felt like my whole body was breaking apart and I couldn't breathe, she trudged into my room and forced me to drink something green that smelt like dirt and eggs.

I made a face after the first sip, but before I could push the drink away, she put her hand on the bottom of the cup and tilted it upward so that I was forced to drink the foul-smelling liquid. It tasted worse than dirt and eggs. When I had finished, I started coughing as I hand-ed the cup back to her. If anything, I felt worse. I wanted to puke, and didn't know if it was because of the drink or because of the secret.

She took the cup and looked at me. I ignored her and fell back down onto the bed, turned onto my side, pulled my knees up to my chest and wrapped my arms around them.

"What, no complaints?"

I shrugged.

She didn't say another word, just left me to myself.

Abuela tortured me for the next few days. She thought she could pull me out of whatever crevice of depression I had fallen into. At first, I was only allowed to eat chicken broth and crackers. I wasn't really hungry, so I didn't care. The following days, she made the dishes I disliked the most: *mole, menudo* and a lot of meals with *nopales.* She knew I hated the slimy texture of the cactus. That was what she was counting on: for me to complain. But I didn't. I didn't have the energy, didn't care. Why should I? School was a blur too. I didn't speak up much in class those days.

She also made me drink that nasty concoction twice a day, morning and night. And I was only allowed to take cold showers, no hot water. She even made me watch *novelas* with Gloria when Saturday came around while she went out to do the rounds.

Even Gloria noticed I wasn't my natural self. "Hey, girl! What's wrong with you?"

"Nothing."

"*¿Nada?* You with your *trompas* frowning all the time and walking around as if everyone should ask you what the matter is. *Mira,* when I was your age . . . " She kept talking but I stopped listening.

After a week, when all that didn't work, Abuela did *una limpia,* a cleansing, on me, because she thought I had *susto,* a disease caused by the loss of soul. For three days in a row, she changed and washed my sheets, replaced them with fresh ones and then placed a cross made of *cenizo* herbs—a purple-colored sage—under my pillow. Before I went to sleep, she made me lie on my stomach while she swept sage over me from head to toe as she recited the Lord's Prayer, and then proceeded to put Holy water on my joints. I had to turn over so she could repeat the process on the front of my body. And to top it all off, I had to drink anise tea with some honey at the end of each sweeping.

I think Abuela was frustrated after the *limpia* was done because nothing happened. I hadn't lost my soul, it was still there inside of me, dormant perhaps but then again I wasn't interested in reviving it yet. You have to want to be cured to be cured. And I just wasn't ready yet. The things we do as *curanderas* don't work if the person doesn't believe, and I didn't believe it could work *for me*. And perhaps, Abuela was blinded herself . . . just like doctors can't treat their own kids. Well, Abuela shouldn't have tried to cure me.

I wasn't sure why I was so upset. Perhaps it was because it was yet another thing I hadn't known about my mother. A *big thing* I hadn't known about her. An older brother or sister? Maybe I was a little jealous. My mother had given birth to someone else besides me. I wasn't the only one in her life or I hadn't always been. And that bothered me.

I had been in my depressive state for almost three winter weeks. Not much of a winter, though: it was still ninety degrees outside. I managed to stay in my slump until Christmas, when Abuela dragged me to midnight Mass in the ugly, green velvet dress that I'd been fitted for those weeks before. I still hadn't said a word to anyone about the secret. Part of me wanted to confront Abuela, and another part wanted to confront Juanita. If I could, I would have confronted my mother. But in the end, I kept it all to myself. It was *my* secret, the only one

I had and if everyone was going to have their secrets, I was going to have mine too, damn it.

Church was a mix of poofy green, red, gold and silver dresses and black, blue, white and brown suits to match. It was always packed, but tonight, the rest of the city who didn't attend Mass regularly was there to get their yearly blessing. And yet, our seats were still waiting for us.

Mass lasted three hours instead of one. There were four baptisms, five catechisms, but Communion took the longest. Hundreds and hundreds of people to be given bread and wine by only three priests, while the rest of us knelt on wooden benches waiting for the lines to end. My knees were numb when we finally stood up. I guess kneeling for almost an hour was supposed to remind us of how Jesus had suffered.

I was now able to get Communion. A month or so before, Abuela took me up to the church on a Saturday. I got baptized in the pool of water to the left of the altar. Then I received my First Holy Communion. I discovered much later that most people have to go through cate-chism classes, but for some reason, I had skipped them.

Since we sat so close to the altar, we were some of the first in line. I didn't like everyone watching me. And I didn't know how I felt about the priest placing a wafer on my tongue. Germs anyone? Still, it was kind of cool being included in this ceremony. Sort of like I was included in Laredo. Like I was Catholic enough . . . even though I didn't really feel like it. I didn't see myself consuming the actual body of Christ. Even though I had experienced some weird things in my *curanderismo* training, that just seemed a step too far. But what was too far in my world? Mostly, my ability to take Communion showed me that at least the Church saw me, recognized what I did with Abuela and how I helped the community.

As we kneeled, waiting for Communion to be over, I watched people walk by us on their way back to their seats. I was supposed to be praying, but I could only pray for so long. As I watched the hundreds of people pass, a woman walked by, her head slightly bent. I might not have noticed her but something about her seemed familiar. It wasn't the way in which she refused to look our way, barely peeking out from the sides of her eyes, then trying to look anywhere but at us. There had been many people who walked by that night that had done exactly the same thing. It seemed half the congregation respected Abuela and the other half feared her. Was this woman scared of the *curanderas*? It didn't seem to be so.

She wasn't a patient. Maybe I had seen her at the market? I couldn't tell because she refused to look at us straight on. Her profile wasn't enough to place her face. As she walked by the pew she tripped on the carpet, stumbling for a second, but still didn't look my way and continued walking. I finally lost sight of her among the other bodies there for Christ's day of birth. I soon forgot about her as I continued studying the rest of the congregation.

By the time Mass finished, my eyes hurt from the glare of the hundreds of burning candles and gold decorations. I was nauseated from smelling the poinsettias, the body odor from a packed hall and from a lack of eating in the last six hours, with the exception of the Communion wafer and a sip of wine. Once we left, Gloria dropped us off at Juanita's. I didn't know where Gloria had gone, but she'd said she had plans and told Abuela to stay out of her business when Abuela asked.

Abuela didn't have Christmas decorations at her house. She said she had them up year round. Statues of Mary, Jesus, Joseph, the manger scene, the three wise men. Very Christmas of her. However, Juanita had the full Christmas set up: fake Christmas tree with lights and ornaments, ribbons hanging on green garland around the doorways, red, white and green candles lit around the house, a plate of cookies, presents beneath the tree and stockings hanging around the door frame because there wasn't a mantle or a fireplace to hang them from.

Juanita had a stocking not only for Abuela but one for me, too. The stocking was green with my name stitched in red. My fingers lingered over the letters of my name.

"I know it's plain, but it's something, right?" Tía Juanita said as she came up beside me and put her arm around my shoulder.

I nodded, trying to swallow the tears in my throat. "My first."

Her arm stiffened at my response. Then she gave my shoulder a little squeeze.

"Thanks," I said as her arm dropped from my shoulder and she walked off. I kept my eyes from hers, not wanting to see her pity. Juanita invited me to stay the night on Christmas Eve. Abuela refused the invitation, saying that her own bed, compared to the one in Juanita's guest room, was better for her back.

I fell asleep on the couch, and in the morning Santa had come. Or that's what my little cousins believed, and I played along. One year, when I was eight, I had woken up in the morning and had run to the living room. We had taped a picture of a Christmas tree I had drawn at school on the wall. I was looking for that *one* present, because usually my mother could afford one small present from Goodwill or some other cheap place, but that year there was nothing except for my mother and some old guy crashed out on the couch. When they awoke, she went to a party with him and left me in the apartment all by myself. She didn't return until a day later.

Most of my Christmases weren't like that, though. Usually, Christmas was boring, and we were stuck in a dingy apartment all day because it was too cold to go outside. Plus we had nowhere to go even if we wanted to leave. But this year, I received presents at Juanita's, and more than one at that.

Aunts and uncles had sent gifts. I got a few shirts, a purse and some make-up from Tía Judith. I probably wouldn't wear it just to make her mad. Tía Judith was always trying to say how pretty I could be if I just had a bit of "rouge." As if anyone had used that word since the fifties. Gloria got me some pencils and a sketchbook. I guess the Devil has a soul.

Abuela gave me a beautiful gold necklace. It had a cross pendant with tiny, golden vines covered in thorns that wrapped around the arms of the cross and came together in the middle where a gold rose bloomed. I fingered the pendant, wondering if she had bought it with my mother in mind. Rosa. Rose.

"Thank you," I said trying to muster the feeling I felt for the gift. It was the nicest thing I had ever owned up until then and definitely the most expensive. It felt odd, considering how numb I had been the past few weeks. Abuela nodded once, looked like she was going to say something but then turned and told Lilia to open another gift. Abuela was never one for a lot of soft emotion.

Everyone watched Lilia and Tomás open presents, not really paying attention to me. I opened a box and found a small, red photo album. On the first page was a picture of the entire family that had been taken one Sunday after church for Tía Perla's birthday. She had insisted she needed an updated picture. I stood to the side of the group between Tía Juanita, who had her arm around me, and Tío Alvino.

I smiled oddly in the photograph, as if I wasn't sure what was happening. Looking at the picture made me smile. I flipped through the pages. The pictures were random ones of me or our family. Many were candid shots, snapped when I didn't know someone was taking a picture. In one picture I was playing with Lilia. In another I was sitting between a few aunts eating a plate of food. I flipped through the pages, smiling. I loved the photographs of the family caught in various moments of laughter or cooking or talking rapidly to one another with hands held out in some explanation of an event. There were even a few pictures of Abuela, who, like me, didn't know the camera was there. She didn't like taking pictures and always turned around when a camera was near.

As I was flipping through, Juanita moved from the couch and sat beside me.

"You like?"

I nodded, "Yeah. This is great. Better than the drawing I did for you."

"Martha, are you kidding me?" She held up the framed drawing I had made a month before of her, my uncle and two cousins. I had drawn Abuela a picture as well, of Mary and Jesus, and was going to give it to her when we got back to the house.

"This is amazing! I didn't know you were so talented," Juanita said.

I shrugged my shoulders. It wasn't too bad.

She smiled. "I'm going to hang it on the wall next to the kitchen so everyone can see how beautifully you drew my little family."

"If you want," I said shrugging again.

"Thank you again, Martha. Hey, flip to the back of the book."

I did as she said, but didn't get far enough, so she flipped the pages for me until she got to the place that she wanted me to see. It was a picture of my mother at the age of seven or eight. She stood awkwardly in a purple dress in front of the church. I flipped to the next. My mother and Juanita sitting on a couch. Juanita was a baby, and my mother held her. My grandfather had his hands under my mother's arms to make sure she didn't drop Juanita. I couldn't see his face; it wasn't in the picture. Abuela must have been the one taking the picture because she wasn't in sight. My mother looked down at Juanita with wonder, tiny lips parted and eyes wide.

Each picture was from a different time, a part of my mother that I hadn't known. I studied the pictures but not for long. I would do that alone in my room for many nights later. Juanita remained silent beside me as I continued flipping pages. Finally, I came to my mother's high school years. She was laughing, posing with her friends, posing with Juanita. The pictures were now taken by friends most likely. I couldn't imagine Abuela being okay with my mother doing a silly pose, kicking her leg in the air like a cheerleader. Abuela would have said *"cochina"* or some other word that would have meant my mother acted inappropriately.

Suddenly I came to a picture with my mother and Sofía. They wore matching tie-dye shirts and each held a hand up to the camera in peace signs. The camera caught them in mid-laugh. Suddenly, Juanita grabbed the album from me. She looked at Abuela, who was watching Tomás open his present. Juanita hurriedly turned the page and handed the album back to me as if nothing had happened. Sometimes my family did too much to keep Abuela from being angry.

I turned the pages, not really caring to say anything to Juanita about what she may have been hiding from Abuela. She didn't say anything either, and a few moments later, she pointed out a picture of her and my mother dressed in matching pink dresses. She laughed as she told me about how the two of them couldn't stop itching in those dresses all day.

I came to a picture with my mother and another woman. They sat smiling in a red booth at a restaurant.

I asked, "Who is that?"

"Carlita, one of your mother's friends."

Carlita looked different from her homecoming picture and the pictures I had found in the yearbook. Her hair was pulled back in a ponytail, and she had blunt cut bangs. I looked at the picture again. Wait a second . . . I had seen her before. I swear I had. But where? It was the woman from church! The one who refused to look at us. How could I not have realized it was Carlita until now? God, I was a freaking idiot! She had been at church, only ten feet in front of me, and I had lost my chance.

My thoughts were interrupted by Abuela. "*¿Qué es eso?*" What is that? she asked. She had stood up and was looking over my shoulder. Her hand was held out for me to give her the album.

I gave it to her without saying a word. So much had happened in a few moments that I didn't know how to respond. She looked at it, at the picture of my mother and Carlita. Abuela's face never changed as her eyes took in the picture. After a few moments, she handed the album back to me.

"I have breakfast to make," she said and walked to the kitchen.

Once

ABUELA WASN'T EXACTLY SURE why I came back to life. I
don't think she really cared why, or even why I had gone
into my small, self-pitying depression in the first place.
She was just happy to have me back. Or as happy as
Abuela could get, which meant ordering me around a little less than usual.

I had a goal once again, something to work toward.
Carlita was the key. She would know what had happened
to the baby, exactly how and why my mother had left,
and maybe even where she was now. So that was my
plan. Find Carlita and ask. It was simple. I already had
addresses that could be hers. I figured it could only be
one of the two addresses closest to the church.

We were still on winter break and more people were
sick. I didn't have time to look for Carlita because
Abuela kept me with her twenty-four hours a day, running errands and administering cures at the houses of
patients while she took care of the ones that came by the
house. Carlita hadn't been back to church.

By New Year's, we were swamped with plastic con-
tainers of *frijoles*, *arroz*, *mole*, *pozole*, *tortillas*, *pollo*, *carne
guisada* and plates and plates of *pan de dulce*. I became
so sick of eating all the food everyone brought us as

thanks and payment that I stopped eating everything but rice and fruit for a few days.

The day before I had to go back to school, Abuela brought out two large canvas bags and threw them on the table next to me. "*Apúrate,* Martha. We go to Mexico today."

I stopped chewing the bread I was eating. Abuela hobbled down the hall and into one of the rooms. She hadn't ever taken me to Mexico. I had my suspicions that she went regularly when I was at school.

Soon after, we drove the Cadillac to a parking lot near the border and then got out to walk on foot. I had the two empty canvas bags draped around my neck. We had to walk up some stairs, then down another set of stairs, then up a few more, until we finally walked onto the bridge. Cars waited bumper to bumper to cross into Mexico, whereas on either side were two sidewalks to allow pedestrians to cross the border on foot. There was a large fence on our right, a means by which to prevent anyone from falling into the Rio Grande.

The sidewalks were crowded with people. On the other side of the car barrier were those returning from Mexico or going to work in Laredo. All sorts of people walked beside us on the path to Mexico. A grandmother with her daughter and her daughter's children walked ahead of us at a slow pace, trying to allow the three little ones with them to walk on their own. We passed men with dirt-stained work pants and buttoned-up plaid shirts who talked with each other of the work they had done overnight on some construction project in the United States. We even saw a few tourists. The Anglos walked with cameras hanging on straps around their necks and sunglasses over their eyes. They smelled like sunscreen, too.

As we walked, I turned to Abuela. "So why are you bringing me to Nuevo Laredo . . . Mexico?"

"You need to know where I get some of my supplies."

"But why?"

"*Ay*, Martha! *¿Por qué? ¿Por qué?* You just need to know, okay? What if I need to send you to get me something?"

Me? Go to Mexico alone? The idea of crossing into another country didn't appeal to me. I'd already crossed into a new country once: Laredo. And I had barely been able to navigate *its* waters. Imagine Mexico, alone. Could I do it again?

There was little chatter as we crossed the bridge, except for the Anglos, who didn't care or notice the lack of conversation. Everyone had somewhere to be, and there wasn't any room for anything that would slow them down.

Only one guard stood on our side. Three faced Mexico on the other side of the bridge. They looked closely at each brown face that walked by, stopping people every once in a while. I'm not sure what the border patrol asked the people they stopped. Sometimes they responded and were allowed to walk on, while other times they pulled out something from their pockets or bags, showed the border men and then continued walking.

Before we got to our guard, one of the other guards on the US side stopped a young woman with a bright pink scrunchie in her hair. Walking ahead of her was an older woman with short, graying hair who was holding the hands of two children, a girl and a boy. The patrolman looked as if he was asking the woman he stopped for papers or identification. She smiled unsurely and looked frantically through her pockets. She turned to the older woman with the two children. The children were trying to look over their shoulders at the pink scrunchie lady, but the woman who held their hands hurried them away.

"Martha, stop staring."

I tripped over Abuela's heels. "Sorry," I said trying to find my balance once again.

"That's their mother, right?"

"*Sí.*"

"Why won't they let her pass?"

"No papers, probably. Mexican citizen." Abuela walked faster, as if trying to put distance between her and my questions.

"But why can't they let her pass? We're going to Mexico, and we aren't Mexican citizens."

"Don't they teach you this in school?"

"No. Are they supposed to?"

"Mexico likes Americans coming in, buying stuff, because we come back home and leave our money behind. Mexicans don't want to leave the United States, and the United States doesn't want Mexicans."

"But why?"

"Why? Why? Why do you care?"

I wasn't sure why I kept asking why. Maybe I just needed to know how a woman would let her kids walk away with someone else, to another country.

"It's just that that woman . . . " I sighed, "Forget I asked."

Abuela kept silent as we walked past the guard and into Mexico.

When we neared the end of the bridge, I spoke again because something had occurred to me. "I don't have papers. How am I going to get back across?" The idea of attempting to return to the United States scared me. Would they believe me? Take me to jail?

"I have your birth certificate."

I stopped, stunned. "Wait . . . what?" Did my mother leave it with her? "How did you get it?"

"I had to pay a man one hundred dollars to get you a new one. I was surprised to discover you were born in Texas."

A new birth certificate? Did she mean that she had my birth certificate reissued or that she got a fake one with my "new" last name, Gonzalez? You never knew with Abuela.

"No worries. They won't even stop us. I know their mothers."

The buildings in Mexico were older and more run-down than those found north of the Rio Grande. As I looked around, I was vaguely left with the sense that Mexico was a blur of brown. Brown buildings, brown streets, with hints of bright colors from banners or signs that swung slowly in the slight breeze. *Cumbias*, *rancheras* and Tejano music fought a cacophonous war high in the air over dominance of our ears.

There were slightly more poor people in Mexico. Children ran toward the Anglos that had walked ahead of us selling chewing gum, pleading, "*¡Un peso, un peso!*" They didn't bother with us.

"Why don't they run at us?" I asked Abuela.

"You want these poor souls to beg you for money?"

I shook my head and looked around. "No, I just noticed they only ran to the *güeros*, not to any of the Mexicans."

"Then you must be Mexican now."

Women and men without teeth or limbs dressed in raggedy clothing sat on the side of the street with signs in Spanish begging for money. Abuela stopped every once in a while, pulled something out of the bag she carried—coins, an orange, a wrapped piece of food, a vial of something—and gave it to some of those we passed.

After about the fifth one, she said, "Too many . . . just too many."

The children were extremely skinny and had round bellies. My mother and I never had it that bad, ever. How could this be? We weren't even a mile from Laredo, and the difference was drastic in the level of poverty. For a moment, I felt nauseated and guilty for the life I had lived, and for complaining about the dingy apartments and hotel rooms my mother had found us.

Abuela led me through brick streets that were as narrow as two people with their arms outstretched. Shops were crammed tightly together on each side of the street. Merchants stood on doorsteps inviting us in or haggling with a customer or two. Abuela walked past them, sometimes she nodded to someone, but mostly she kept on straight. I, on the other hand, kept finding myself trailing behind. Each food cart we passed made my mouth water. Mexico smelled like a mixture of dust and spicy food. It was the oddest thing.

I was fascinated by all that was being sold. Bright clothes, books, spices, food, statues, liquor . . . It was a market with everything you needed, for mere *pesos*.

When Abuela told me that one dollar equaled almost seven pesos, I freaked out. I could be rich in Mexico.

Five minutes later I said, "I'm a little surprised."

"At what?"

"I thought Mexico was going to be a lot different from Laredo, but it really isn't."

She shrugged. "I guess that's why they call it 'Nuevo Laredo.'"

We finally came to a small alcove of shops down a side street. Our destination was the last shop on the left, squished between a shop full of perfumes and one that sold old cassette tapes and played *ranchera* music on a portable stereo, the kind of stereo that was as tall as your knee caps and as heavy as a bag full of bricks.

The shop we entered was compact and smelled like Heaven, if Heaven had a smell. I entered a thick cloud of aromas: dried plants, herbs and sharp, stinging spices. Oddly enough, the one spice that stood out among the others was cinnamon. My senses were overloaded, so much so that I felt my body go woozy and my eyes closed for a second. I loved it. Abuela's *curandera* room was only a small taste of the rich perfume that permeated the shop.

Thousands of clear jars neatly lined the shelves that had been built into the walls. There were small scoopers and bags so that customers could pack their various purchases separately. There were even small weighing stations set up on tables. My fingers itched to touch everything, open up every jar and discover how I could use all the hidden treasures. The brightness in the shop made me look up. In the ceiling, an old, plastic skylight let in the Mexico sun for a natural brightness.

Abuela left me and went straight to the shelves to get things I assumed we were short on. When I finally got my bearings, I caught up to her. She already had three small bags filled.

"What's that?" I asked pointing to a jar filled to the top with a gooey substance. Inside the gooey substance were objects of some sort. I moved closer. It was a . . .

"Is that a baby mouse?" I asked.

Abuela nodded, with a small smile.

"Please tell me we are not getting that today."

"Well, I wasn't planning on it, but stick your hand in there and get one. Never know when it might be useful."

I looked at her in disgust, and she responded with a laugh.

After collecting some reddish powder, another grainy, tan powder and dried petals from a jar, Abuela finally went to the cash register, where a young woman with long, dark hair, smooth, caramel skin and big eyes stood. She was the most beautiful person I had seen since we had entered Mexico, although, when she smiled at Abuela, I noticed that her right front tooth overlapped the left one.

"*Buenas,* María. How are things?"

"Good, Margarita. This is my granddaughter, Martha. Martha, say 'hello.'"

"*Mucho gusto.*" Nice to meet you, I replied.

"*Igualmente.*" Margarita put our purchases on a scale.

"How's your family? Your sister, is she still having problems?" Abuela asked Margarita.

"The family is good. Healthy and strong. As for my sister, she will be all right. Nothing a few teas, protection and prayer can't cure."

Margarita must have been a *curandera,* too. Why have all these ingredients if you didn't know how to use them? She rang up the prices, and Abuela handed her some dollar bills and waved her hand when Margarita took the bills to indicate that she did not need change.

I moved to the door to leave but stopped when Margarita said, "María, I wanted to tell you. A young woman from your side came in the other day . . . looking for herbs."

Abuela asked, "What kind of herbs?"

"*Bruja* kind."

"She say what for?"

"I didn't ask. Who knows if she even knows how to use them, but has that ever stopped anyone? "

"Did you get her name?" Abuela's white, caterpillar eyebrows pulled together, lips pursed.

"No. She handed me the money and ran off. Very rude. But if I had to say, she was about your granddaughter's age. A little shorter. Too much make-up."

A chill ran beneath my skin and the hairs on my arms stood up.

"I'll watch out for this girl. Thank you, Margarita," Abuela said as she walked past me and out the door.

Part of me wanted to ask Abuela if it was Marcela. Every time Marcela came up, though, the tables turned and I was the one being scolded for something or another. Regardless, if she had those herbs, it couldn't be for anything good, right? And how would she even know what to do with them? And what were they exactly?

Too many questions that needed answers—as if I didn't have enough questions already.

As we walked back to the border, I suddenly noticed something. It was quiet outside. There were a few people mingling, but for the most part, the streets were bare, and many shops had closed their doors.

"Where is everyone?"

"Siesta," Abuela replied.

¿Siesta? That didn't make sense. "It can't be. That's around two in the afternoon. It's only ten in the morning, if that."

Abuela only responded by pointing her finger to a clock tower up ahead: 2:14 p.m.

"How . . . " I couldn't finish the sentence. We had lost at least four hours in the shop, when it seemed we spent no more than ten minutes . . . twenty at most!

Abuela said, "Don't think about it."

And I didn't. I couldn't. How can you think about losing four hours in ten minutes? You couldn't. That's *loco*.

Doce

I RETURNED TO SCHOOL the second week in January with mixed emotions. Part of me was sad because I had enjoyed only working with Abuela over the break. Now that I was back at school, I would be overloaded once again with homework *and* healing responsibilities. Another part of me was apprehensive. Marcela's suspension was over, and I imagined she would be more pissed at me than she was before. That morning, when the brick building of the school came into sight, I prayed that somehow, someway, I'd be spared Marcela for the entire semester if not for the rest of my life.

Either I wasn't praying correctly or God didn't hear me, because the first person I saw as soon as I walked into my first period was Marcela sitting in the back row. She sat in the far right corner, looking ahead at the blackboard. No one spoke to her. For that matter, no one sat at the desks in front or beside her. Everyone sat closer to the door and did their best not to look her way.

She looked at me as soon as I walked in, and her eyes grew dark. She turned away and looked out the window, but her hands gripped the edges of her desk—she was not happy. Neither was I. I sat down in the front row, first seat, closest to the door, as far from Marcela as I possibly could. And still, I felt too close.

What was she doing in my class? This was an Advanced English class, and Marcela only took regular classes. Did she miraculously grow a brain and hoped to get into college or something? I didn't see that happening in my lifetime.

It was the most excruciating hour of the day. I tried to look forward and listen to the teacher, but the entire time I felt Marcela's eyes boring into me with all the ways she wanted to gut me. After a while I started to picture all the creative ways Marcela could kill me: stab me with a sharp pencil in the throat, knife to the back, slam my head into the tiled floor a few times, perhaps? I wanted so desperately to turn and give her the finger or a mean sneer, but it wouldn't help my situation. It'd probably set Marcela off, and then somehow Abuela would magically hear about it, and—*bam!*—I'd be the one in trouble.

At lunch, I looked for Laura so I could ask her about Marcela, but I didn't have a chance. When I sat down, Laura was already gossiping with the twins, Bella and Estrella. They were seniors like Laura.

"Can you believe it? I bet her mother had a fit when she found out," Estrella said.

"Yeah, well, can you imagine? Her favorite daughter pregnant? My mom would have hit me, too!" Bella added.

My ears perked up. "Who's pregnant?"

Bella and Estrella looked at me as if I was a two-headed alien. They didn't really like me since Laura had included me at their lunch table. I didn't like them either. They gossiped too much and liked to laugh at other people's misfortunes.

Laura turned to me. "Leta is."

"Who's that?"

"Freshman . . . Leta Gallos."

Oh, shit. Señora Gallos, her daughter. I hadn't told anyone. Actually I had sort of forgotten about her when I figured out my mother had had another baby. God, I was selfish. "How did it get out?" I asked

"Her mother found her trying to take a piss test! What a *tonta*. That's why you do that stuff at school," Bella said.

Poor Leta. Pregnant, just like my mother.

Laura and the twins continued to speak about Leta.

A little while later, I interrupted them. "Do you guys know why Marcela is in Advanced English?"

"I heard no other English teacher would allow her in their class. Mr. Martin's brave, if you ask me." Bella said.

Or stupid, I thought.

"Well, I heard her mom's making her take the class," Estrella countered.

I didn't continue the conversation, and no one else seemed to want to either. The twins moved on to gossiping about who might have gotten Leta pregnant. Laura watched me for a few seconds, chewing at her lip as if she wanted to say something, but she never did.

I ate my food, not really in the mood for any part of the twins' conversation.

At the end of lunch, a short guy walked up to our table.

"Laura Valdez?" He asked.

Laura turned to him. "That's me."

"The office sent me. Your mom called and needs you to call her back at the store. It's important."

Laura rolled her eyes. "Probably needs me to come in after school." She picked up her Styrofoam tray. "I'll talk to you guys later," she said as she followed the boy.

Valdez. Laura's mother. It stuck in my head and pounded at my temples. The pregnant Gallos girl. No, that couldn't be it. I looked at Laura. She was almost out the cafeteria door. Someone called to her. She looked and waved. No, it *couldn't* be Laura. Could it?

"Damn, Martha. Looks like you've seen a ghost," Estrella said. "Marcela threatening you again?"

I shook my head.

No, but I think I had figured out how Sofía had helped my mother: Laura. She had raised Laura for her.

I managed to stay out of Marcela's way the first day and even the first week. She continued to give me the death stare each morning in class. That wasn't my biggest concern, though. Laura was. Was Laura my sister? Had Sofía taken my mother's baby and raised it herself? Was that why Abuela didn't like Sofía? Didn't really want me to hang out with Laura?

Each day at lunch, I watched Laura, trying to see my mother in her. But each time I looked, I just didn't see it. Maybe I didn't want to see it. I didn't look like my mother, either. Laura did have Jorge's widow's peak. Then again, Laura didn't look like anyone in the family, not even her own mother or Abuela. Sofía had curly hair and Laura's was straight . . . like my mother's.

I didn't mention my suspicions to Laura. I mean, how do you do that? "Hey, Laura, I think we are sisters"?

I needed more information. Carlita. She was the key. The key to knowing exactly what had happened and if Laura was who I thought she was.

Even though the Laura question laid heavily on my mind, I had other things that kept popping up in my life and kept me occupied. Like how Marcela stopped coming to school. Well, sort of. The second week of school—Friday—I came into class without looking in Marcela's corner, as had become my habit. It wasn't until class was halfway through that I noticed I hadn't felt the prickly feeling working its way up my spine. I turned around and found Marcela wasn't in her seat. I didn't see her the rest of that day anywhere else at school, either. The next week she missed two days: Wednesday and Friday. A few days the next week, and the next and so on.

Eventually, she only showed up two or three days a week. Part of me was relieved. It was as if God had heard my prayer in some way. If only I could be satisfied with the silence that greeted our English teacher when he called out Marcela's name. But I wasn't. I couldn't stop wondering where she was.

My gut told me that the girl that Margarita had spoken of was Marcela. Who else wanted power? Who else would go looking for it?

I tried to ask around as quietly as possible. There were ears and eyes everywhere in my school, as I had come to find out. Everyone I asked had no idea where she was, much less what she was doing. Some said she skipped with her gang to smoke weed. Others said she had a job across the border at a taco stand. And one person had heard she was selling drugs or making them. They were all pretty far-fetched to me, but this was Marcela we were talking about. Who knew?

The next two months went by in a blur with healing and school. And yet, two things occurred around the end of February that renewed my interest in my mother—not that she had ever left my mind exactly. Every day I ate lunch with Laura was a day of scrutinizing every expression she made: her hair, her eyes, the way she spoke and what she talked about. I just needed to see the connection between her and my mother.

I had to.

On a Thursday night, I had just taken a shower and returned to my room to lie down. I was exhausted. For some reason, my mother had plagued my mind all day. There wasn't anything in particular that had made me think of her. It had begun as soon as I awoke, and it nagged me each hour and throughout the day.

During her teaching once, Abuela said to trust these nagging feelings. They meant something. I asked her what but she just shrugged and said, "Who knows? But when I pay attention to them, they seem to help me. Sometimes they save lives."

When the feeling wouldn't go away, I got a crazy idea. I grabbed a few candles and put them on the small dresser. I stood in front of the candles and closed my eyes and dug within my memory for a picture of my mother. Finally, I found it: a memory of her when she worked at the breakfast diner in Orlando. She looked down at me with an actual smile, not one of her Big Fakes, as she sat a plate of pancakes in front of me.

I then prayed. Attending church and learning to heal had given me some kind of faith that I wasn't quite sure of, but I found myself believing the prayers I said sometimes. Maybe there was a God and a Jesus listening to me. I prayed mostly because it felt comforting to think that someone listened, knew my troubles and helped me to heal.

But now, I prayed for my mother. Not anything as specific as health or safety, I just prayed with her in my mind, and before I ended I asked God to let me discover what had happened to her and where to find her. When I opened my eyes I saw that the candles were lit. I stepped back in surprise, turned around and peeked down the hall. Abuela was in her room. I turned back to the candles. Had I done that? I hadn't lit them, but somehow a flame flickered back and forth on each wick. These candles had a life of their own. I looked once more at them suspiciously, then hopped into bed.

When I woke up the next morning, they were still lit.

Two days later, Gloria brought over some *enchiladas verdes* that she had bought from some lady at church who was selling them to raise money for her son to go to college. Abuela made *frijoles* and *arroz* to go with them.

I took my first bite and couldn't help myself. "God, these are *so* good."

Gloria snapped her fingers two inches from my nose, "Hey, watch your mouth, *chica*!"

I stuck out my tongue when Gloria looked down to take a bite, but Abuela caught me.

"Clean the dishes after dinner and water the plants."

My punishment. I fought not to argue back and nodded instead. They took the "Don't say God's name in vain" commandment way too seriously.

I ate silently, as did Abuela, while Gloria talked, which was pretty normal. She never shut up. Literally never. She was going on about some scandal in the neighborhood: Señora Ramírez, the one who lived in the orange house, not the white house, had caught her husband cheating on her with her own sister.

"You'll probably have to go over there in a few days. Calm them down, cure their marriage. *Más problemas.* I told them that . . . " The phone rang, cutting off Gloria.

We stopped eating and looked at each other. We never got any phone calls at this hour. We were more likely to get a knock on the door.

It rang again. Gloria and Abuela looked at me for a few seconds. I looked back confused. Finally, it dawned on me: they wanted me to answer the phone. I got up.

"Hello?"

No one responded, but someone gasped quietly.

"Hello?" I asked again.

No response. I turned and shrugged at Abuela and Gloria. Gloria was looking at me, but Abuela was not. Her back stiffened and her head tilted toward her plate. The next second, she let out a sigh, and her body heaved with a release of tension. A second later, she started eating again.

Something about that movement triggered a memory.

I gripped the phone tighter. "Mom?" I whispered into the phone.

No response, only breathing.

I whispered, "Can you hear me? Where are you? Mom?"

The silence stretched between the lines. I closed my eyes and reached through the phone with my *don,* a desperate attempt. It was all I could think of. I sent it out like I did when I healed. I wasn't even sure it would work. Through the phone I heard another gasp and then a click.

I slammed the phone against the receiver. The phone fell off the receiver and hung by its cord. Clenching my fists tightly, I fought not to hit the wall. One breath. Two. Three. I picked up the phone and placed it on the receiver a little more softly, even though I wanted to slam it about five more times.

When I returned to the table, I didn't look at Gloria and I couldn't look at Abuela. I only looked at their plates. Abuela was almost done. I picked up the fork and began eating again, not tasting the cheesy, spicy deliciousness of the enchiladas any longer. Gloria picked up her fork too.

I would have been happy to finish the meal in silence, but of course, Gloria did not allow it.

"Humph," she paused, "that was pleasant . . . *Más problemas*, like I was saying . . . " And she continued with the story about the cheating husband between mouthfuls.

Later, I realized it was the first time I could ever remember calling my mother, "Mom."

Trece

ONE TUESDAY IN MARCH I returned home from school later than usual because I had Statistics tutoring. My body dragged itself through the living room and into the kitchen. I hadn't been getting much sleep, and the effects were pounding my body. Every night for the last few weeks, I had tossed and turned in bed, wondering and wondering. *Where was my mother? Who was the baby? What happened?*

The aroma of *caldo* met me in the living room and was confirmed when I found Abuela standing in front of the stove, dropping pieces of chicken into a boiling pot.

"Someone sick?" I asked throwing my bag down next to the wall.

Abuela sighed in a way that said she was displeased that I had just thrown my bag on the floor. I pretended I didn't see and sat down.

"Why does someone have to be sick? We prevent sickness, just as we heal."

Whatever. I was too tired to ask what she meant. I relaxed into the chair, glad to be home and able to rest for just a moment before Abuela sent me to the healing room to clean, or prepare something, or before she made me do my homework, which I dreaded. Statistics and an essay. Kill me now. But for a moment, no thinking, just . . .

"Martha!" I jumped and almost fell out of the chair. Damn. I had fallen asleep.

A bowl of soup had been placed on the table for me, and Abuela stood next to me with a look of satisfaction on her face.

"See? Prevent!" She turned around, grabbed her own bowl and sat down on the other side of the table. I hated when she was right.

Gloria wasn't eating with us tonight, not that I minded. I could only handle a certain number of her snide comments. Probably as many as she could handle of my sarcastic ones.

We ate in silence, but spoonfuls away from finishing, Abuela spoke. "I have a cousin that lives in Mexico."

I paused, the spoonful of soup halfway to my mouth. "Okay."

She pursed her lips and continued. "My cousin has a daughter who is about to birth twin boys, and they want me there when the children come."

"Okay . . . " I repeated. What was the problem? Mexico was only a few blocks over.

"*Ay*, Martha! Enough 'okay,' 'okay.' Can I finish already?"

"I thought you wanted me to say something." I guess I couldn't do anything right. I brought the bowl to my mouth to slurp the last bit of soup . . . loudly.

"If I had . . . never mind! *Stop* slurping! They don't live across the border. They live about eight hours in. I will be gone two days. And because of school . . . "

My ears perked up. I tried not to show my excitement with a smile or worse: interest in the fact that Abuela would be gone for two days. And the best part: I'd be alone—two days of paradise in Laredo, or the closest damn thing to paradise in Laredo anyway. I was never left alone in this burning hole. Abuela or Gloria were always around.

I tried to maintain my cool. "Okay." Simple, sweet, and it didn't divert from my previous responses. I even added a nonchalant shrug for effect. After setting the bowl down, I grabbed a piece of bread from the center of the table and started breaking it apart and eating it.

"I don't know if I should . . . "

No, she couldn't do this to me. "Why not? Don't *not* go because of me."

"That's exactly why I wouldn't go."

I pinched my eyebrows together. "What do you think I'm going to do?"

She set her spoon down. "Something. Nothing. Anything could happen."

I rolled my eyes. "Anything could always happen."

She picked her spoon up and began to eat again. She didn't speak when she finished her soup, and she didn't say anything else as she gathered the bowls to wash. I itched with anticipation. What was she going to do? I would have usually left the table, but tonight, I lagged behind. I had to hear her decision before I left.

By the time she was done washing the dishes, she still hadn't said anything, and I was restless. Guess it wasn't going to happen. I got up from the table and began to walk to the hall. All at once, the noise in the kitchen stopped. I paused and turned around. She wasn't moving and she didn't turn around when she spoke.

"Okay. I will go. But Gloria will come over every night to cook."

"I did feed myself before I came here, you know."

"Gloria comes, or I do not go."

"Fine, fine. That'll be fine." I cringed at the thought of a few meals alone with Gloria.

"Make sure nothing happens."

I didn't reply.

Time to find Carlita.

Abuela had not told me the exact day she would leave. Two days passed and nothing. It was excruciating. I looked over all the information I had on Carlita. I had three addresses. I would start with the closest and work my way to the farthest.

Finally on Friday morning, as I was getting ready for school, Abuela came into my room.

"I will leave today and will be back early Sunday morning for Mass."

Of course. Abuela wouldn't miss Mass. I had been standing on one leg, trying to balance as I put on my last sneaker when she said this. I was so caught off guard by her announcement that I fell back toward the bed.

"Oh . . . okay," I said as I awkwardly laced up my sneaker, one leg held up in the air while lying on my back on the bed. "So what time are you leaving?" Shoes tied, I stood up.

"Gloria will pick me up soon and take me to the bus station."

I nodded in response.

Abuela's eyes narrowed. "Don't think you won't work while I'm gone. There are some cures in the work room. Give them to Señora Alvarez, Señor Luna and Señora Reyes this afternoon. You will make rounds on Saturday morning. That is all you are to do. When you finish, return here to this house and stay."

Stay. As if I was a dog. I nodded my head like an obedient pup. I wasn't about to do anything that would make Abuela change her mind.

I grabbed my backpack. "Okay. I have to get to school."

We stood there. Abuela looked at me suspiciously, but then again, when did she not?

"Well . . . safe travels," I said, hesitated, then walked past her, through the house and out the door. As I walked down the front porch steps, I paused. Maybe I should have given her a hug or something?

Right. Give Abuela a hug? She would have never left if I had done that, convinced I would do something horrible behind her back. I started walking again. What I had planned wasn't all that horrible. I needed answers, and if Abuela wouldn't give me the answers, then I had to find them myself. So going behind her back to find out about my mother, well, it was partially Abuela's fault as far as I could see.

As I walked to school, I planned out my rendezvous. I couldn't search for Carlita after school. Abuela's patients would be waiting at the house for their cures. If any of them didn't find me there, they'd call Gloria, and Gloria would make it her life goal to see that Abuela tanned my brown hide when she returned. So that left me with two options: to search for Carlita tomorrow—on Saturday—after my rounds, or begin today and skip school.

I was taking a big risk if I skipped school. My absence would be immediately noted and someone, actually a lot of someones, would probably make it their mission to tell Abuela. Everyone knew her, and I knew she'd be checking up on me regardless of the fact that she'd be in another country. She knew things that were impossible to know, like what I ate for lunch or the fact that I once took two bathroom breaks in a class period.

So was it worth it? Was skipping out on school and finding Carlita worth it? The school came into view, as did hundreds of teenagers. Buses and cars lined the street in front to drop off kids. From one of the cars, a woman jumped out and yelled at a boy who walked toward the school. She waved a brown paper sack in the air at him. I couldn't hear what she said, but it was obvious. The kid had forgotten his lunch.

The son, or I assumed it was her son, ran back to his mother, grabbed the sack, gave her a kiss on the cheek and turned around to run to the school, where a group of boys waited for him. The mother put her hands on her hips and shook her head, then turned and walked back to her car.

That kid knew where his mother was. She probably didn't keep major secrets from him. Didn't I deserve the same thing? I couldn't wait another day. Finding Carlita was worth everything, and if that meant I had to suffer the wrath of Abuela when she returned, just for skipping part of school, it would be worth it. I hoped.

After entering the building, I ran into Laura on the way to class, which wasn't unusual. Her homeroom was across the hall from mine.

"Hey, Martha. What's going on?"

I walked a little faster. "What do you mean?"

She looked at me oddly and walked faster to keep up. "Well, I was just being polite, but now . . . I can see something is up. What is it?"

I shrugged. "Nothing. Just stuff on my mind."

"Yeah, me too. My mom won't give me a freaking day off from the store lately. I *do* have a life. Did I tell you I got accepted into Houston? Partial scholarship, though."

We came to our rooms and stopped. "That's great. Partial is better than nothing, right? Congratulations," I said.

Laura had a future—college next year, and a career would come after that. Was it right to tell her about her past?

She smiled then said, "Thanks. Hey, you sure you're okay?"

I readjusted my backpack. "Yeah, I'm good. But . . . "

"But what?"

This was probably a bad idea. "Look, there's something I have to tell you soon. Just not now."

"Is it bad?"

How to answer that? "I don't think so." My gut said otherwise. "Look, I'll tell you later, okay? Got to get to class."

Laura waved awkwardly, pursing her lips to the side and pinching her eyebrows in confusion. I couldn't think about *her* right now. Leave it for later.

When I sat down at my desk, I decided I would leave after lunch to find Carlita. I was going to do this for me and for Laura. When class started, I looked over my shoulder.

Marcela was absent that morning. Again.

Catorce

MY EXCITEMENT about skipping school and finding Carlita rushed into my legs, and I practically ran to the first house on the list. Yet, when I came to the house, I stopped. There must be a mistake. There were two houses, one on each side of where the house should have been, but nothing in between except a dirt lot with patches of dry grass. I ran back and forth between the two houses looking at the numbers. 1606 and 1610. Where was 1608? I kicked at the ground and stubbed my toe. "*¡Mierda!*"

I pulled out the map and looked to the next address from my jean short's pocket. No time to waste. The next house was five miles away. What I wouldn't give for a car. I looked at my watch. It was 1:00 p.m. That meant I had only a few hours to get to the next house and back to Abuela's. I took off at a jog. This was not starting out well.

It took me an hour to get there. As soon as I hit the street, I slowed down. Cameron Street. The house number was 1414. Unlike most of the colorful houses that surrounded it, this house was grey with white shutters.

I stood in the street looking up at it. At least there was a house, which meant there might be a person there . . . that's if Carlita didn't have a job and was actually at home. I should have thought about that before. Great.

I walked up to the house with a cramping stomach and a sweat-drenched shirt.

Someone was yelling inside, but I couldn't hear what they said. I didn't have time to wonder because the door swung open, leaving only the screen door between me and what looked like a woman on the other side. Her features were indiscernible due to the darkness from inside the house and the screen door that obscured her face.

"She's to have no visitors. She's done with you."

"What?" I said.

"You can't hear? I said, *leave*! She's not going to hang around you or your friends anymore."

"I'm sorry . . . I don't know what you are talking about." I patted my hair down. Who did she think I was?

The woman stepped closer, and still I could not distinguish her face.

"You're not here for my daughter? Not one of those gang members?"

I shook my head. "No. I'm just looking for Carlita Juárez."

"Oh." She opened the screen door. "That's me. Well, it was me. I'm married now."

And it *was* her: Carlita, the woman from church. She recognized me too. Her eyes shifted and looked behind me, like a mouse fearing a nearby hawk ready to snatch it from the ground.

Carlita regained her composure, stepped out of the house and closed the door behind her.

"Why are you here?" she whispered harshly.

I wasn't sure why she whispered, but I responded normally. This was it. "I, um, I wanted to ask you about my mother."

She crossed her arms. "I don't know where she is. You need to leave. Your *abuela* wouldn't want you here."

"Why?"

"I don't know. Sorry, but you must go."

I shook my head. I wasn't going anywhere until I got some answers. "No. Maybe you don't know where she is, but I want . . ." I paused. *You can say this. Just say it.* " . . . to know about the baby."

Carlita's body tensed and her face lost its color. "You know about that?"

I nodded.

"How?"

"Does it matter? I just want to know what happened. Did my mother have it or . . . give it to someone maybe?"

"Why would you say that?" Her words were sharp, and she had stopped whispering now.

Something told me not to say anything about Laura. "It's a logical explanation. Adoption, maybe?"

She shook her head, not wanting to meet my eyes. "I can't say. Now you must leave, please. Those things are secrets for reasons."

"I could just ask Sofía."

Carlita's head whipped up. "Don't you dare! Even if you do, you think she'll tell you and suffer your *abuela*'s wrath? Go for it. Sofía isn't as stupid as she may look."

I didn't know how to respond but I didn't have to. Behind me sounded the roaring motor of a truck coming near and the lyrics of "Thunderstruck" by AC/DC. Carlita's eyes widened. I turned around. The motor died down, and a man stepped out of the white truck. No way! It was Jorge Valdez.

"Why is he here?"

She opened her mouth but no sound came out. I felt Jorge walk up beside me a moment later.

His forehead wrinkled and then hardened. "Why are *you* here? No, I don't care. You must leave," he said.

"Leave?" My neck became hot, and my fists clenched. What the hell was going on? "Not yet. Why are *you* here?" The question hung in the air and was answered when he looked away. "Are you two . . .?"

Jorge didn't respond.

I looked at Carlita. "You're married?"

She might have answered if it wasn't for someone coming to the door from inside the house.

"Mom, is that Dad? I . . . what the hell are you doing here?" The screen door opened and out stepped Marcela from the darkness of the house.

I looked at Marcela and then at Carlita. No. How could that be?

"Cela!" Carlita said, but Marcela ignored her.

They didn't even look alike.

"I said, why are you here?"

Marcela's eyes grew black as she stepped forward.

Marcela, Carlita. Marcela, Carlita. Marcela was eighteen. My mother was pregnant eighteen years ago with Jorge's child. Jorge was married to Carlita now. Oh, shit. . . .

"No. No. Are you kidding me?" My body was tensed so tightly that my arms began to shake.

"Don't . . . " Jorge began to say and reached out to me. I stepped out of his reach.

"Don't what? Are you kidding me?" I pointed at Marcela, who now looked more confused than angry.

"What's she talking about?" Marcela asked her parents without looking away from me.

Carlita pleaded with her eyes. Anger flushed across my chest, directly beneath my skin. I was burning up. This went beyond the scorching heat of Laredo.

"So this . . . she's it? The truth?" I asked.

Carlita didn't nod. Carlita didn't say yes or no, but the lines of her face, even the smallest movement of her eyes spoke volumes. *Sí*, yes. It didn't matter what language it was. It was the truth.

I turned, ran off the porch and down the street in the direction I had come. Neither Carlita nor Jorge tried to stop me. They wanted me to run, away from them, away from Marcela so I wouldn't continue speaking.

Yet, footsteps sounded behind me.

"Hey! Where do you think you're going?"

I kept running, just a few seconds more, until I felt a push from behind. I stumbled but caught myself, stopped and turned to look at Marcela. Couldn't she just leave it alone? I was saving her from the truth, trying to run from it myself. Couldn't she see that? I was trying to save her! But if this was how she wanted it, well then, that's how it would be. But before I knew it, I was sent flying backwards and slammed into the concrete ground.

For one second, I didn't hear anything, didn't feel anything, only saw Marcela's face close to mine, her teeth bared, that black fire burning in her eyes, lips pulled back in a snarl like some wild animal attacking its prey. And then she hit me. I felt that.

The blow to my face sent more than just pain. I felt my skin burn and the center of my chest ignite with fire. She had used her *don*. The fire spread out through my body directly beneath my skin. It was my dream . . . the dream I had had the first time after I had seen Marcela, my first night in Laredo. I was burning alive in her black flames.

I couldn't let that stop me. After she hit me, she tried to grab my throat with both hands. If I didn't fight I would turn to ash. Through the pain, I clawed at her arms and grabbed the left one, yanking it so that she fell off me for just a moment. I scrambled to her and swung my right hand, balling it into a fist at the last moment. It hit her on the side of her head. After that, we were a mess of kicks and slaps and punches, and I didn't feel any of them because my skin burned. I think I was screaming but I can't be too sure. I can't even tell you if she screamed or yelled.

I wasn't able to have a clear thought, except one: *Make her hurt*. And so I did. I opened the gates and let the water run. I found the spot deep within my chest and sent my *don* out through my hands, the force of which sent us flying apart, me skidding across the concrete a few feet away. The fire stopped, and now all I felt was the skin on my arm ripped open by the concrete and aching with pain from Marcela's kicks and punches.

Forgotten were Abuela's words: "Never use your *don* to harm." It was no different from healing a patient—direct my *don* at the disease—and send my power.

I looked up. Marcela was moving to sit up.

"Leave it alone, Marcela!" I yelled through gritted teeth.

Carlita and Jorge jogged toward us. What they hoped to stop was already well beyond their control.

"You bitch," she groaned.

I didn't give a damn anymore about the right or wrong thing to do. I wanted Marcela to hurt just as badly as I did in that moment, and it would take more than a physical or spiritual battle to do that.

I pointed at Carlita, who was only a few yards behind Marcela and coming closer by the second. "That woman? Your mom? Think again. She's a liar."

Marcela didn't respond, but she didn't have to. She pushed back her hair as she struggled to stand. I followed slowly. There was a flash of pain in my right ankle when I put pressure on it.

"That woman isn't your mother," I said, hopping up on my left foot.

"Shut up, you lying whore." Marcela held her ribs with one hand.

"Ask her." This was not who I was . . . an insensitive brat who wished pain on others. But my hate and anger consumed me beyond the point of caring.

Marcela didn't speak, just breathed heavily, trying to catch her breath. We stared at each other, and then Marcela turned around and looked at Carlita. I couldn't see Marcela's face but I could see Carlita's, and there was no way that Marcela could deny the truth now.

"Carlita is just the lady that *my* mother dumped you with." There. I had said it. She got what she wanted.

Carlita and Jorge had stopped running and now stood ten feet from Marcela, obviously not sure what to do. Carlita was crying, and Jorge looked like a man who had lost everything—pain and sorrow etched into his face. I couldn't see Marcela's face . . . but I saw something else. Marcela's *don*. She had used it on me moments earlier and it was growing around her, dark purple and blue mixing to form a smoky source of energy.

I had seen this in Abuela when she healed, the growing of power before it was sent out into the patient, so I knew Marcela was about to throw her *don* toward me at full force. She didn't need to touch me to hurt me. She could do it at a distance. This wasn't the school yard fight we had been engaging in a few moments ago. This was her using a mystical knife that would pierce deep into my gut.

I don't know why I didn't stop it. I think I could have. I was bewitched by Marcela's power, how mad she was, how hurt she was . . . . She was dying inside.

When her power hit me, I didn't feel anything. Nothing. I was nothing. I was nowhere. It was peaceful . . . for just one tiny second. And then it was all there; it was everywhere. Her power was fire and it was burning. I felt every vein, every skin cell, every organ burning away.

My vision blurred until Marcela became only a dark human-like shape.

I felt the flames lick my legs, singe my arms and wrap me in their embrace. I was burning in her anger, burning in her pain, burning in the knowledge that she was my sister.

That was when the screaming began.

Quince

THE SCREAMING WOULDN'T STOP. It just kept going on and on. It was worse than the fire burning me up. So much worse.

Through the screams I heard a faint but familiar tune: *My spirit is crying for leaving.*

It was so hard to hear with all that screaming.

In my thoughts I have seen rings of smoke through the trees.

If the screaming could just stop, I could deal with the fire. It was a part of me now, burning everywhere. But it couldn't be stopped.

And the voices of those who stand looking.

"Martha!" A man's voice cut off the tune. "Martha! Look at me, Martha!"

I was moving, bumping up and down. My eyes opened.

"Martha!" Jorge yelled again. "Martha, listen to me."

He was driving fast, I think. I was lying next to him. We were in the truck. He touched me. The fire burned hotter, the screaming got louder. And I fell back into the flames.

"Tell her to come now!" Was that Gloria?

Something was coming up. A burning ball of fire up my throat. I needed . . . I needed. . . . Fire burst from my mouth.

"She's throwing up now! And the screaming!"

Something slammed. Gloria turned me over onto my back. The pain was overwhelming. I was going away again.

"They're coming, Martha! They're coming!"

It was eating me, eating me alive. Pulsing. Taking over my blood. I was being exterminated. It was yellow, orange, then red, until finally it turned a bright blue and burst into a white hot flame across my body.

A hand touched me.

Don't touch me. Don't.

Rubbing now. That was worse. It was touching my arms, spreading. It wasn't stopping. Make it stop!

"Gloria, please, help me," a slow, deep voice said.

"What do you think I'm doi . . . " Gloria grunted.

I had to tell them to stop. Don't. Except . . . wait, was the fire going away? No, it was there. It was leaving the surface and burrowing deeper. It was going for my *don*.

The fire cleared from my eyes and, for one moment, I saw Señor Díaz. He was crying.

Don't cry, I said. Or did I?

The tears were running down his face so fast. *So fast.* He caught them in his hands and poured them over me. Tears to extinguish the fire.

It's not working, I said. Or did I? I couldn't tell because I had . . . had to . . .

"I'm here!" Abuela's voice rang out.

It won't work, I told her.

She was crying, too. No, that couldn't be right.

Gloria moved out of the way, and Abuela kneeled next to me. Her hands were over me. The fire didn't like that. It pushed back. The screams started again.

Abuela closed her eyes. Her face was a map of worry, fear and sweat.

I told her not to worry. It was okay. Or I think I did.

"Tell her to come now. Not tomorrow. Now!" Abuela yelled.

Gloria said, "What if she won't listen?"

"If she dies, I'll . . . I'll . . . "

She dies. She dies. She dies.

The fire wiped away any notion of time. It could have happened for days or weeks, for all I knew. I wasn't fully aware of much beyond my pain. Or maybe I was, but I was no longer sure what was reality and what wasn't anymore. The fire and the burning had become my reality.

I heard things. The fire spoke to me. It told me of its plans to possess me, to burn me up from the inside out. I tried to look for where it hid within me. If I found it. Could I fight it off with my *don*? The screams persisted.

During this time, I saw Abuela in the flames. She told me to push my *don* upward and out, to push it up until it touched hers. I think I tried. It helped some. Or maybe it didn't.

Later or earlier, who knows, Abuela told me stories about herself. She told me of her brothers and sisters. She described her mother's cooking. She painted a picture of the small village where her father's family was from. There was a lake. I tried to jump in. Abuela said to try. But the flames held me back.

I almost accepted the fire, accepted that it would be there with me for the rest of my life. Then something happened. It changed. The fire wasn't so hot anymore. That was the day my mother showed up in the flames. She didn't say anything, just stood there looking at me. We regarded each other. The fire moved away from us and, for the first time in a while, I could breathe without my lungs crumbling to ash.

I walked toward her, my feet burning on the hot coals of the secrets that I had just learned. Her lips spread into the Big Fake but they didn't stop spreading out over her face and then down her body until the person who stood there was not my mother, but Marcela.

Marcela jumped when she saw me. She did a double-take, then beheld my fiery cell. "No! No, no, no, no," she said.

She turned to walk away but as she did, my mother appeared and Marcela bumped into her. Marcela stumbled back and looked up at my mother, who no longer had the Big Fake on her face. My mother was looking at Marcela. I couldn't tell what she was thinking. Was she mad? Sad? Upset?

"What do you want? Move out of my way!" Marcela yelled.

I don't think Marcela knew who she was.

My mother turned around and grabbed something. A metal pail. She handed it to Marcela, who nearly dropped it. Water sloshed out when she caught it. When Marcela stood up again, my mother was no longer in front of her.

"Where'd she go?" Marcela said.

I wasn't sure if she was asking me or just speaking aloud. I almost told Marcela that she was gone, maybe

she was never there. I might have said that, if I didn't
hear my mother urging me, "Martha, wake up." I felt the
ghost of her lips on my cheek and I was suddenly hurled
into a black tunnel.

It took me a second to realize the screaming had
stopped.

Dieciséis

I WOKE UP CHOKING AND SPUTTERING. My mouth tasted like salt. When I finally stopped, I realized that I was awake, like *awake*-awake. There was no fire. No burning.

There wasn't much time to consider how I had woken up before I realized that Gloria was yelling for Abuela.

"María! Come, quick! She's awake!"

Gloria did the sign of the cross and then pushed back the hair on my forehead. "You stupid, stupid girl. *¡Gracias a Dios!* You're alive. I can see it in your eyes."

I wanted to ask if I had died, but instead croaked. "Water?"

As Gloria stood up, Abuela rushed through the door. Or something that looked like Abuela. She had lost weight in her face and around her stomach. There were shades of purple beneath her eyes, and her hair seemed thinner. What happened?

I moved to sit up, but Abuela, who had quickly come to my side, pushed me down. "No, no. Lie down. There. You're not ready to get up yet."

Gloria handed Abuela a cup of water, and Abuela put it to my lips to drink. Everything in my mouth felt dry. For that matter, my whole body suddenly felt dry to me, and my skin bristled with each movement.

"Thanks," I said and laid my head back down, suddenly feeling very tired, so tired that I fell back to sleep.

When I woke up again, Abuela was sitting next to me in a chair. Her head was drooped forward and her chin was on her chest, which rose and fell steadily as she slept. I took a second to look at her again. I hadn't hallucinated before. She looked bad, bad as in old. Like really, *really* old.

I must have made some kind of noise, because she woke up, cleared her throat and rubbed her hand over her eyes.

"You're awake," she said.

"You too," I replied.

She nodded her head slowly. "How do you feel?"

I hadn't thought about it. Without thinking, I reached out with my *don* across my body. My body was tired but I was fine. There was no more fire.

"It's gone. The . . . the . . . "

"A curse," Abuela finished for me.

"No. That . . . a curse? But it burned. I . . . I felt myself burning."

Abuela nodded. "That is what some curses do."

I tried to push myself up on my elbows, but Abuela gently pushed me back down, which was probably for the best because I realized quickly that I didn't even *have* the strength to get up.

"Don't rush it," she said.

"But how did I get a curse?"

And suddenly, I remembered it all. Marcela was my sister. My mother was her mother. The fight.

"Marcela did it. She hit me with a curse."

Abuela's body stiffened. "Yes," she managed to spit out between her clenched teeth.

"Because she's my sister."

Abuela slapped her hands together. The sound was so loud that I flinched. "She is *not* your sister!"

Abuela was breathing hard and turned to look across the room at the wall.

"What would you call her? My mother gave birth to her, so I'm pretty sure that makes her my sister. You knew about this?"

She had to have known about Marcela. Abuela turned and pointed at me. "That is none of your business."

"I'd say it is, since she almost killed me." Okay, yelling made me dizzy.

"But she didn't!"

"She could have, thanks to you! If I had only known . . . "

"If you had only stopped asking questions. . . . You go behind my back, searching like a detective or something, asking people questions."

"You never told me anything!" A few black spots appeared in my vision.

"Because you didn't need to know," Abuela said. "That girl has nothing to do with you. If you had only minded your own business, this would not have happened."

I laid down. "Why keep it a secret? What were you so ashamed of?" I said quietly, no longer having the strength to yell.

Abuela swallowed hard, and we stared at each other for a few more seconds before she stood up and walked out the door.

I slowly turned over onto my side and curled my legs up to my chest. I had the right to ask those questions, I knew I did, but for some reason I felt like I should feel bad about asking them. Maybe I felt guilty for yelling at her. Whatever it was, I didn't like it.

I had fallen asleep again. When I woke up, I was still lying on my side and somehow I knew I wasn't alone. It was Abuela. She was behind me, but I didn't want to turn to look at her.

"I know you're awake," she said.

I still didn't want to turn over and look at her, so I remained facing away.

"Fine. You don't need to look at me, but you will listen."

She paused for a long time. I almost turned over to see if she was still there, when she finally spoke again.

"I wasn't a bad mother, but your mother wasn't the easiest to raise. She had a future, a gift. A *don* like yours. But she never listened and was always talking back to me . . . And then she started dating that boy. I warned her. She had been with me when we delivered the babies of the other young girls who didn't listen to *their* mothers. She knew what could happen. But she didn't listen.

"Ro . . . " Abuela couldn't even say her name. "Your mother wasn't even going to tell me that she was pregnant. As if I couldn't tell. I . . . I didn't know how to bring it up, though. When we finally talked about it, it didn't go over well."

She paused again, and I wondered what Abuela's face looked like right then. Was she crying? Did she look sad?

"She couldn't keep the baby. Your mother wasn't ready for that responsibility."

I turned over quickly to look her in the eye. "So you made her give up Marcela?"

Abuela squirmed in her chair and glanced away for a second. "I don't want to hear you say that name."

"Why? What does it matter?"

Abuela pursed her lips. "The only sensible thing that your mother ever did was to listen to me and give up that child."

Her words felt like a knife through my chest. Maybe she saw my face because she suddenly realized what she had said.

"Martha, I didn't mean . . . Leaving you here . . . I . . . "

"Why would you say that? It's like you don't even care what you did to my mother, Marcela . . . " Abuela started to open her mouth. "Me!"

It was quiet. She didn't know how to explain herself.

"Look," she finally said, "you may not like what happened, but I just wanted you to know that these things are more complicated than they seem and how they happened. You may not like how they happened, but I won't apologize for my part in them."

"Fine," I said and turned away from her. I wanted to argue more, but what was the point?

I heard Abuela's chair squeak as she stood up. She started walking to the door.

I don't know why I said it, but I should have kept quiet. "She came back for me."

"Who did?" Abuela said.

"My mother," I said, still looking away. "I saw . . . felt . . . her. She made the fire go away."

Abuela sighed. "Martha, she didn't come back. I made the fire go away."

No, that wasn't true. It couldn't be. My mother wouldn't have shown up in my dream for no reason. I had felt her kiss me on my cheek, just like I had felt Abuela's hands touch me when she tried to make the fire leave. Why would she say that my mother hadn't come back?

"I don't believe you," I muttered.

Abuela didn't respond.

Diecisiete

ABUELA DIDN'T COME to my room for the next two days. Gloria did, which was worse.

When she first came in, she said, "I swear, Martha, if you were my granddaughter . . . "

I almost replied, "but I'm not," but thought better of it, because she was the one holding my food. She fed me all my meals, which mostly consisted of chicken soup and water. I didn't care. I was ravenous.

"Slow down. You'd think you haven't eaten in three weeks," she said when I slurped down each spoonful of my first meal quickly.

"How long was I out?" I asked.

"Two weeks."

During those two weeks, the news of my "illness" had spread around town. I hadn't noticed before but the cot that I was lying on in Abuela's workshop was surrounded by flowers and plants and a couple of homemade cards. I think they had lit candles for me too because the faint smell of smoke and incense permeated the room. The church had also gotten involved.

"You must thank everyone. The church, too. You know how many prayers have been said for you?" Gloria tsk'd. "You need to thank everyone in person. Every single one."

"Fine, just give me another spoonful of soup!" I wanted to scream at her.

Obviously, Gloria wasn't the best company to have after suffering from a curse for two weeks.

On the third day, I received a good surprise in the form of Señor Díaz.

"Wake up, wake up." He tickled my nose.

I opened my eyes and smiled. "Hi."

"Good to see you, *m'ija*."

I liked when he called me that. "Good to see you, too."

"Feeling any better?" he asked.

"Immensely. Thanks for helping out."

"You remember?"

I sat up so that I could see him better. The wrinkles in his face seemed softer than the last time I saw him. A flash of tears streaming down his face popped into my head. "I think so."

He smiled. "Have you stood up yet?"

"Just to go to the bathroom. But Gloria is usually there to help me walk."

"Well, let's see if you can do it on your own now. Yes?"

He held his hand out to me. I pushed off the thin blanket that covered my legs and moved my feet toward the ground.

I grabbed his long, spiny brown fingers and tried to push myself up, but my legs just felt weak. Before I could fall back onto the cot, Señor Díaz pulled me up with more strength than I thought he possessed.

It was a little too fast though. I felt my head go woozy with the movement.

"You all right?" he asked.

I nodded.

"Don't lie to me."

I held onto his shoulder for support while his hands held my shoulders steady. "Just a little bit too quickly."

"It'll pass," he said.

He was right. Even though I felt weak, I could stand now. I let go of his shoulder, righted my feet and stood on my own. "I think I'm good now."

Señor Díaz let go of my shoulders. "Walk around the room."

I did. Walking was a lot easier than it had been that first day with Gloria.

When I returned to Señor Díaz, he clapped twice. "Good job. Now take these." He bent down, reached into his knapsack and pulled out two jars filled with a green paste. He handed them to me. Medicine?

"This is going to taste bad, huh?"

He chuckled. "I would think so. It's soap."

I looked at the green goo a bit closer. "Oh, thanks."

"Well, get going." He cocked his head to the door. He must have seen the confused look on my face because he explained, "Martha, it's been over ten days."

I blushed and moved faster than I probably should have for the door.

After my shower, I opened the door slowly and looked down the hallway. No Abuela. I thought a lot as I had taken the shower: she was the reason my mother had left. She made her give up Marcela. She lied to me this whole time and would never have told me about my sister—that sounded weird—except that I had found out! I used to think she was mean, but this was beyond anything that I could grasp. And it left me at a loss, so much so that I washed my hair twice by accident.

I just couldn't figure out why she would do all of this. It wasn't for me. It was for her.

Before I could make it to my bedroom (I had decided it was time to sleep in my own bed from now on and not the cot), I heard Señor Díaz's voice from the kitchen.

"She will come around."

"Will she?" asked Abuela. "Would you? I know I wouldn't. And what if she's like me?"

There was a pause and then a loud clang, as if Abuela had dropped something into the sink.

"Is that so bad?"

Abuela interrupted him, "So it will always be like this."

"María, she's not exactly like you," he added. "She is her own person and still very young. This is a lot to deal with."

"I can't apologize for something I do not believe in apologizing for," Abuela said.

"Even if it means her forgiving you?"

I waited. I waited. I waited some more. Answer already, Abuela!

"No. I cannot. It is not who I am." More pots scraped and clanged.

"Then you must not apologize, if that is who you are. Martha just hasn't discovered what's bothering her."

Abuela chuckled. "I feel like you're actually saying I should apologize."

He laughed too. "All I'm saying is that it's hard for children like Martha to be confronted with the fact that their parents are not perfect."

"She already knew that about her mother," Abuela replied.

"I wasn't talking about her mother. I was talking about you."

I stopped listening and quietly shut my door.

For the next few hours I stayed in bed, hands behind my head and thought about things. At one point, I heard Señor Díaz leave. Mostly, I thought about my mother. My mother who had had so many secrets. It was as if getting pregnant with Marcela . . . that was weird to think about. But I had to. Marcela was my sister. *My sister.* I grimaced.

I wondered where she was. Gloria said that Marcela had run off and no one knew where.

"Probably doing *bruja* work for one of the cartels. *Desgraciada,*" were Gloria's exact words. Being a witch for a cartel sounded far-fetched to me. If I was her, I'd go looking for my mother . . . our mother . . . whatever.

I laid there and wished I hadn't started looking for my mother. If I hadn't, I wouldn't have discovered everything. But at the same time, it felt like . . . this was meant to have happened, one way or another.

Besides, this wasn't my fault. It was Abuela's. All of this led back to her.

Señor Díaz was wrong. She wasn't my "mother." I had a mother, and she was a piece of work. Granted, Abuela had done more for me than my mother ever had: she cooked, washed my clothes, helped me with my Spanish, taught me how to tap into my *don*, and . . . well, she saved my life. Maybe.

But that was the problem! If she hadn't done all of that nice stuff, been good to me, I wouldn't be so mad, so hurt. I didn't deserve this!

I balled my hands into fists and threw them forward so they hit the bed. I just still couldn't believe Abuela. She betrayed me! After all these months, teaching me how to be a *curandera* . . . and then she kept my mother and Marcela from me! She preached honesty and being good and praying to God . . . and she lied!

My mother lied about everything, too. She didn't know any other way. But Abuela was supposed to be different. She was supposed to be better. Morals, ethics . . . that's what all of these stupid Jesus and Mary statues were about, right?

I groaned and looked up. Bloody Jesus looked down at me with sad eyes. A drop of plastic blood dripped from the bottom of his heel. It hung in the air, attached to his foot, forever unable to fall on my pillow.

"Bloody Jesus," I whispered. "What should I do?"

Three loud knocks on my door was my answer.

"Jesus!" I yelped and nearly fell off the bed.

The door opened and in walked Gloria. Her facial expression was one of suspicion. "Are you feeling bad again? That *maleficio* come back?"

"No, you just scared the . . . I mean, you scared me," I said, getting to my feet.

She nodded and put her bony hands on her hips. "See, I thought I heard you take the son of God's name in vain, but you would only do that if you were raving sick again, right?" Her eyes squinted at me waiting for an answer.

I fought not to roll my eyes. "Yeah. That'd be the only reason," I said with a little too much sarcasm.

Gloria pursed her lips and raised her hand as if she wanted to say more, but she shook her head and motioned instead toward the door with her hand. "*Vamos*, dinner's almost ready."

Oh, no. I wasn't going to sit in the dining room with Abuela and Gloria. I'd pass on *all* that awkwardness.

I wrapped my arms around my stomach and scrunched my face in slight pain. "You know what? I actually don't feel so great. Think I'm going to just lay down tonight . . . skip dinner."

I tried to move toward the bed, but Gloria, as old as she was, was quicker and slapped the bed with her open hand. "*Ay*, no! Get your little butt in that kitchen, *chica*. I didn't nurse you for months . . . "

"It was two weeks . . . ."

" . . . for you to lie in bed and die. You've slept enough. Now, you eat," Gloria finished.

She turned and started walking toward the hall, probably seeing on my face that I had lost the battle. I dragged my feet reluctantly after her.

When we got to the kitchen, Gloria pointed to the table and told me to sit. I thought about barking, but I didn't think anyone would find it funny.

I tried not to look at Abuela at the stove top, stirring something in a pot. It smelled like browning rice . . . just a hint of something burning. She didn't turn around to look at me either, which was fine. I didn't have anything to say to her either way.

Which didn't mean that Gloria didn't have anything to talk about. She could have a conversation with a rock if she needed to.

"Like I was saying, I went to the base yesterday to get my hair done. The ladies up there do it best. I don't know how they do it, but I walk away with most of my hair. These other places, they give you a girl who don't know nothing about hair. Burn it right off your scalp."

Abuela stopped stirring to pour a bowl of water in the pan. Steam hissed and crackled from the pot and enveloped the area around her face. She went over to a cutting board and grabbed a knife to start slicing tomatoes and peppers.

"Anyways, I see Lidia . . . the one married to Pablo—not Lalo—Pablo. Anyways, Pablo passed away a few days ago . . . *Dios*, may he rest in peace. She was there getting her hair done for the funeral. She tells me her husband was a good man, but he had a drinking problem."

Abuela stopped chopping for a moment and looked down. After a few seconds, she started again.

"But a drinking problem he gave his son! See, Lidia, the poor soul, can't find her son. Not since she told him that his father passed . . . something to do with his heart . . . I don't remember. Maybe it was something else. But anyways . . . "

Abuela stopped again. This time she switched the knife to her left hand and squeezed the right a few times, opening and closing her fingers. If I hadn't slightly been paying attention, I wouldn't have noticed that she sent part of her *don* to her hand.

"So she sends out her brothers to all the bars, this side and across the river, and nothing. Nothing at all. What kind of son abandons his mother, especially in this hard time? Was it the father who took care of his son? Lidia held the family together. I mean, as best a woman who smokes too much can, at least in my opinion."

Abuela started chopping again, but after a few seconds the knife clattered to the counter and then to the floor.

"So as I'm sitting there . . . " Gloria stopped.

I stood up without thinking and picked up the knife. As I did, I caught sight of Abuela's hand. It was contorted and twitching. She quickly hid it behind her apron when she saw me. I picked up the knife, and she held out her left hand without looking at me.

I looked at her left hand and noticed it looked fine. No twitching. I stood up and mumbled, "I'll finish."

Abuela stood there when I moved to the cutting board to finish cutting the tomatoes. She didn't seem to know what to do. I could feel Gloria's prying eyes watching us, trying to figure out what we would do. When I felt Abuela's presence move away from me and her feet shuffle to the table, Gloria began talking again.

"You won't believe it. While we were there in the salon, her daughter walks in and says they've found him—Lidia's son. You won't believe where he was at."

As I chopped, I wondered about what I had seen. Was there something wrong with Abuela? I had never seen that before. Was it just arthritis or something more?

"He was at the cemetery!" Gloria cackled and slapped the table.

I picked up the cutting board and moved to the stove. As I did, I looked at Abuela. She was sitting at the table, not looking at me or at Gloria, just straight ahead. Her hands sat on the table in front of her. Fat fingers rubbed the swollen knuckles of each hand, back and forth.

"He'd been there for days . . . lying on the exact area his father would be buried in. Can you believe it? He wasn't much of a son, but at least he made it to the funeral."

I finished the *arroz con pollo*, the same meal Abuela had made me almost nine months or so ago when I first came to stay with her. I gave everyone a plate before sitting down myself.

During the entire meal, I watched Abuela, or tried to, without her knowing that I was watching. She didn't look that old a few weeks ago. The age spots on her cheeks seemed to be spreading and her saggy cheeks looked parched for water. The skin on the front of her neck seemed to droop even more. Was her hand shaking as it carried pieces of chicken and rice to her mouth, or had I imagined it?

She wasn't young like my mother. She wasn't even as young as Gloria, though knowing Gloria, the crone would outlive us all anyway, even with her chain-smoking habit.

I was suddenly reminded of something Abuela had once said, that some healings could hurt a *curandera*, even kill them. Was that what had happened, what was happening? Had the curse done this to her?

"Oh, I forgot to tell you, María," Gloria said. "Do you know what Lidia's son said when they found him? 'I won't believe he's dead. I won't.'" She shook her head and ate a piece of chicken.

I couldn't finish my meal. Before anyone could say anything, I stood up and cleaned my dish, putting the leftovers aside to be eaten the next day. I cleaned the dishes when Gloria and Abuela had finished eating.

Gloria left soon after that, telling me, "Glad you're feeling better, *m'ija*."

I couldn't tell if it was sarcastic or sincere. The woman had moods like the Texas weather: calm and sunny one minute and pounding hail and pouring rain the next.

Abuela walked Gloria out of the house. I waited for her to come back in, but I didn't hear the door. I stood in the kitchen with a towel in my hand, twisting and squeezing it. I thought about the year I had had: how Abuela had kept a huge secret from me. How I was abandoned. How I had lived through a curse of all things, and hadn't died even though I remembered begging to for many days.

I thought about how Abuela had looked weeks ago when she had left for Mexico and how she looked now.

My chest felt tight all of a sudden and I walked to the front porch, telling myself I needed air. When I opened the front door, I saw Abuela sitting on the bench pushed up against the house, looking out at the street, at nothing really. Her hands sat in her lap, interlaced, knuckles round and shiny. A large strip of pink paint drooped off the house right next to her ear but she didn't seem to notice.

I slowly walked to the bench and sat down next to her. I felt her body stiffen and heard her take a quick hard breath through her nose.

Following her gaze I saw a neighborhood that I had once been so scared of: brown children, lifeless lawns, colorful houses sighing with age and a shimmering wave of heat that weighed down on everything. I thought about the house that was behind us, how it stood out among the others but still sagged, peeled and grew older.

I glanced at Abuela out the corner of my eye. She was pursing her lips and then relaxing them as if she wanted to say something. But she never did. Instead, she pursed her lips some more, rubbed her knuckles in her lap and stared straight ahead. She didn't notice the few flecks of Pepto-Bismol-colored paint that fell onto her shoulder and into her white hair.

Tentatively, I reached out and covered her hands with my left hand, sending a wave of my *don* to her knuckles, hoping to ease the pain of the secrets that we had suffered.